Maysoh

HANAZUKI

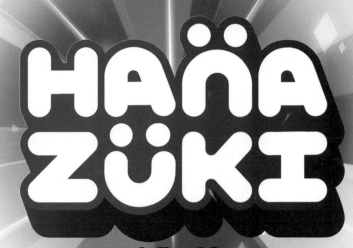

full of treasures

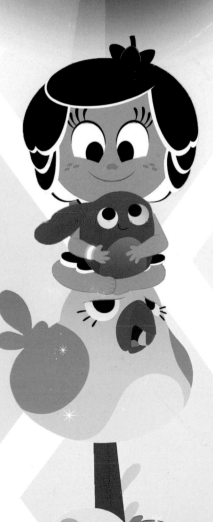

full of treasures

Become our fan on Facebook **facebook.com/idwpublishing**
Follow us on Twitter **@idwpublishing**
Subscribe to us on YouTube **youtube.com/idwpublishing**
See what's new on Tumblr **tumblr.idwpublishing.com**
Check us out on Instagram **instagram.com/idwpublishing**

IDW
www.IDWPUBLISHING.com

Licensed By:
Hasbro

Ted Adams, CEO & Publisher
Greg Goldstein, President & COO
Robbie Robbins, EVP/Sr. Graphic Artist
Chris Ryall, Chief Creative Officer
David Hedgecock, Editor-in-Chief
Laurie Windrow, Sr. VP of Sales & Marketing
Matthew Ruzicka, CPA, Chief Financial Officer
Lorelei Bunjes, VP of Digital Services
Jerry Bennington, VP of New Product Development

21 20 19 18   1 2 3 4

ISBN: 978-1-68405-102-1

Originally published as HANAZUKI: FULL OF TREASURES issues #1–3.

For international rights, contact licensing@idwpublishing.com

ADAPTED BY
DAVID MARIOTTE

ART BY
NICO PEÑA

COLORS BY
VALENTINA PINTO

LETTERS BY
CHRISTA MIESNER

SERIES EDITS BY
DAVID HEDGECOCK

COVER ART BY
NICO PEÑA

COLLECTION EDITS BY
JUSTIN EISINGER AND **ALONZO SIMON**

COLLECTION DESIGN BY
CLAUDIA CHONG

PUBLISHER
TED ADAMS

BASED ON HANAZUKI
EPISODE 1 WRITTEN BY DAVE POLSKY
EPISODE 2 WRITTEN BY KARA LEE BURK
EPISODE 3 WRITTEN BY ERIC ACOSTA

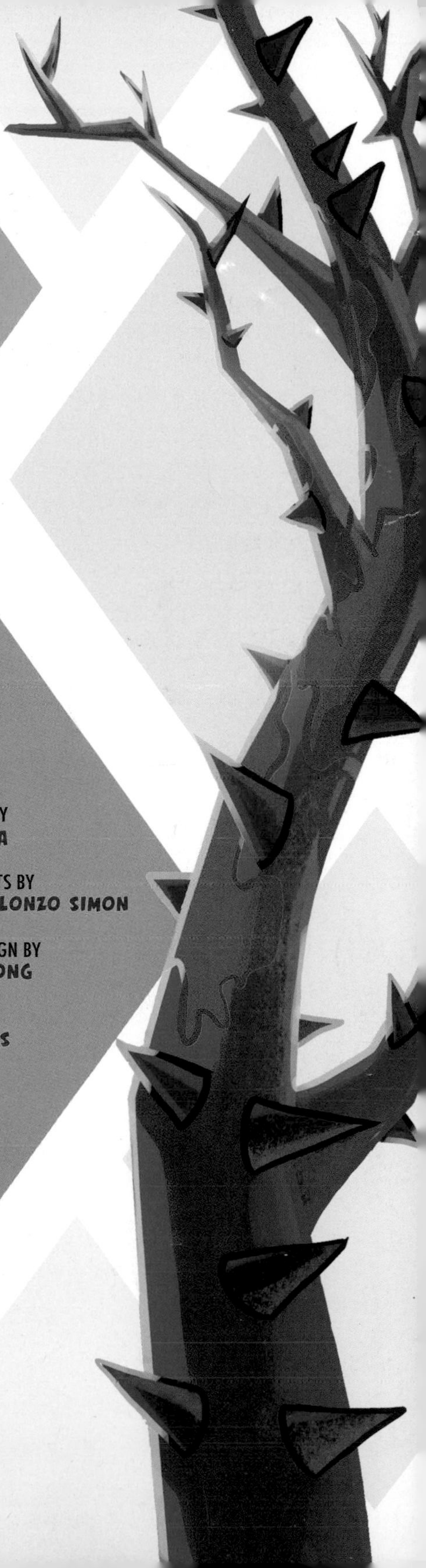

COVER ART BY **CHRISTINA ELLIS**

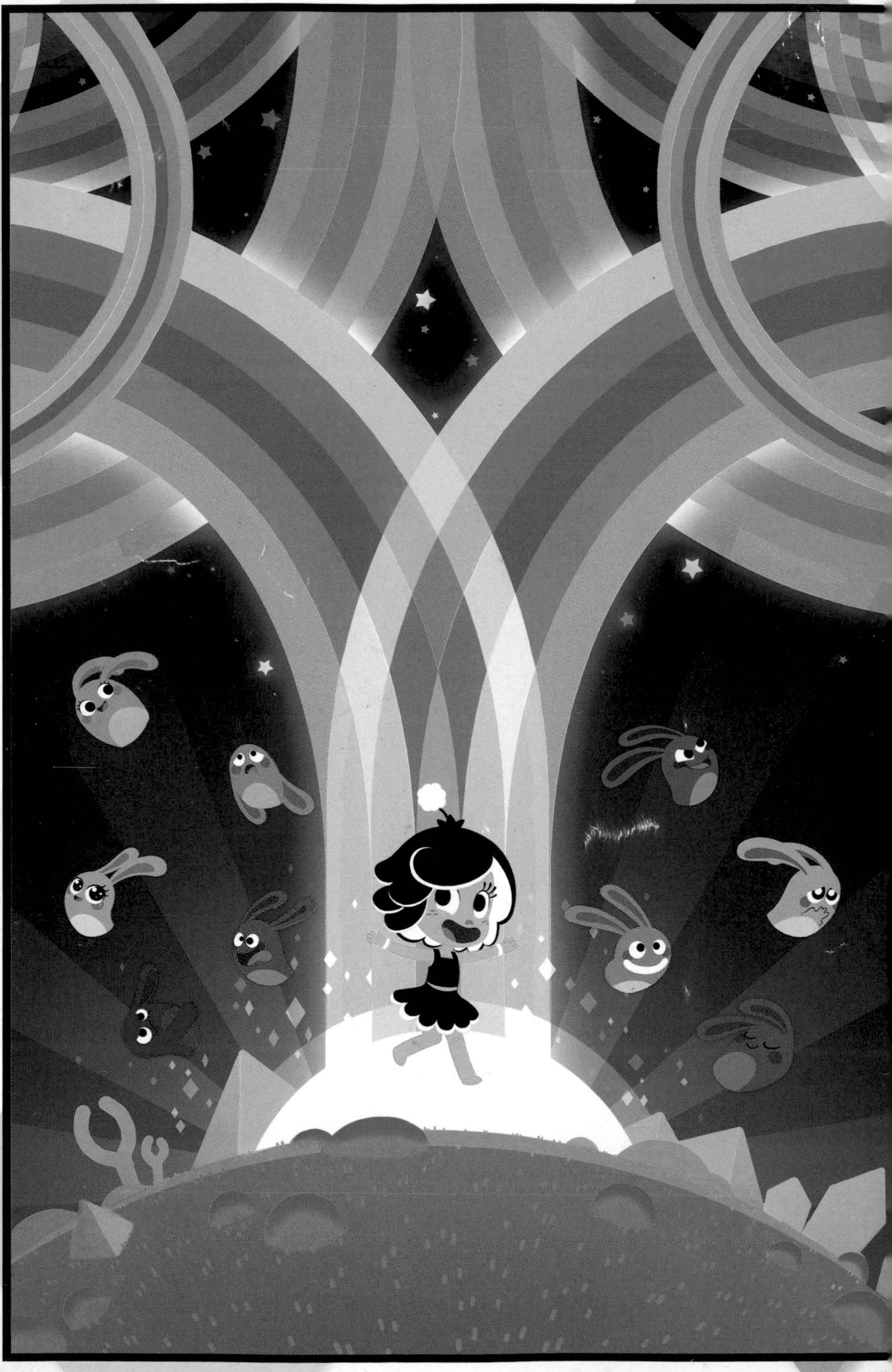

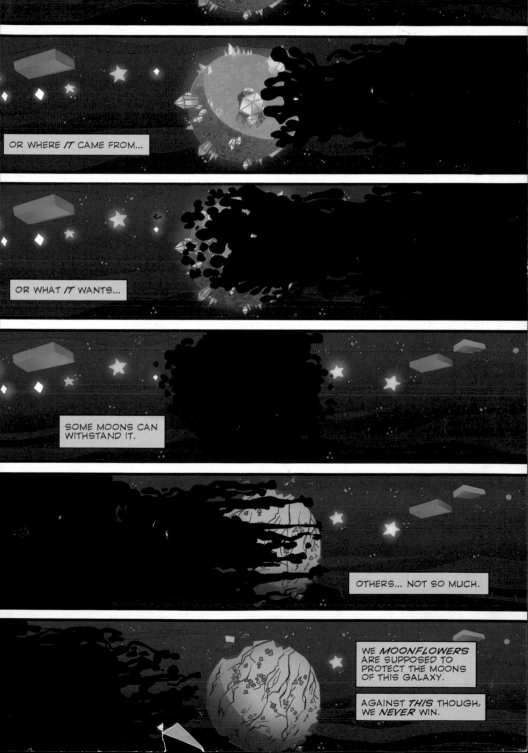

NO ONE'S SURE WHAT *IT* IS.

A MOONFLOWER IS BORN

OR WHERE *IT* CAME FROM...

OR WHAT *IT* WANTS...

SOME MOONS CAN WITHSTAND IT.

OTHERS... NOT SO MUCH.

WE *MOONFLOWERS* ARE SUPPOSED TO PROTECT THE MOONS OF THIS GALAXY.

AGAINST *THIS* THOUGH, WE *NEVER* WIN.

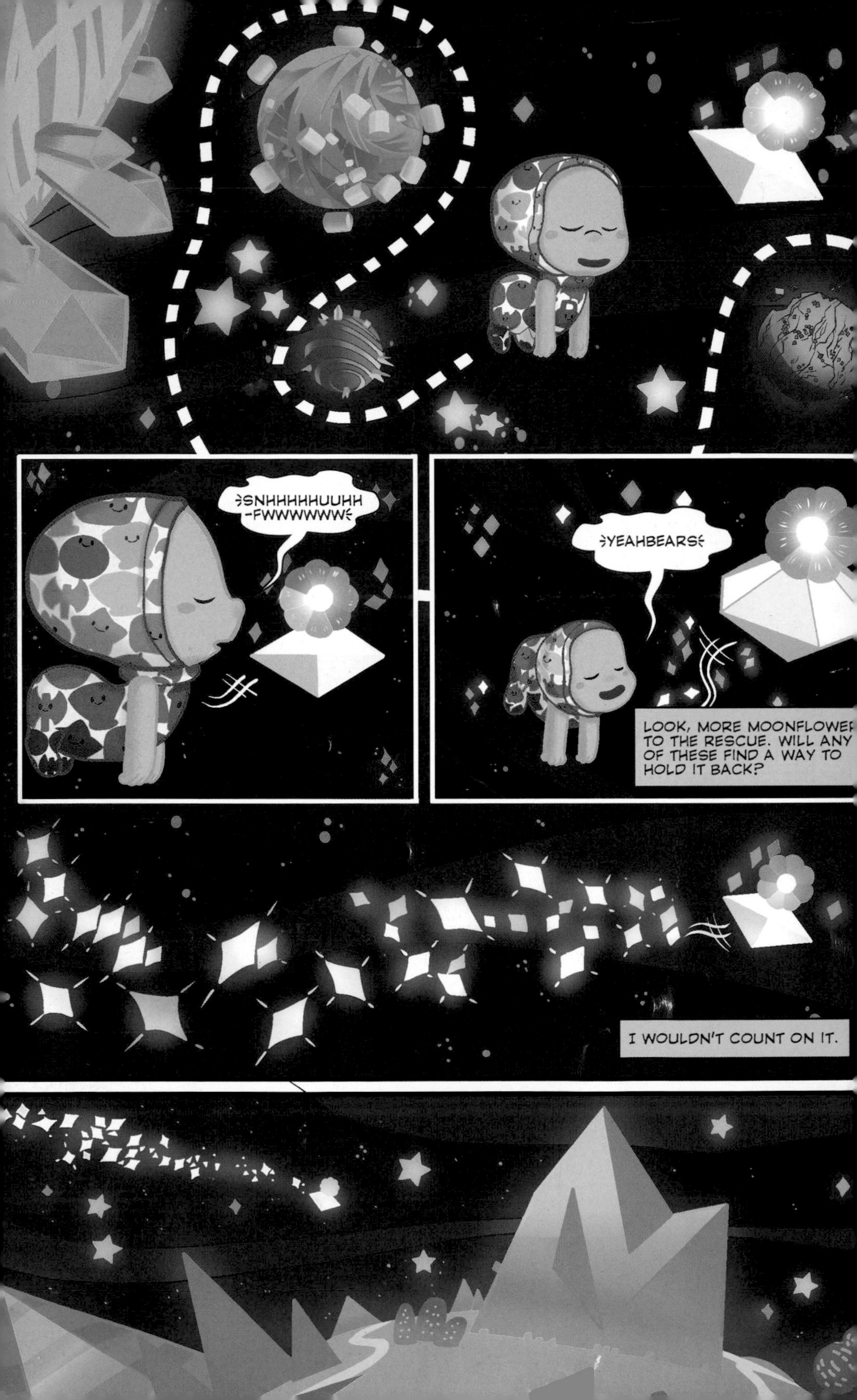
SNHHHHHUUHH -FWWWWWW
YEAHBEARS
LOOK, MORE MOONFLOWER TO THE RESCUE. WILL ANY OF THESE FIND A WAY TO HOLD IT BACK?
I WOULDN'T COUNT ON IT.

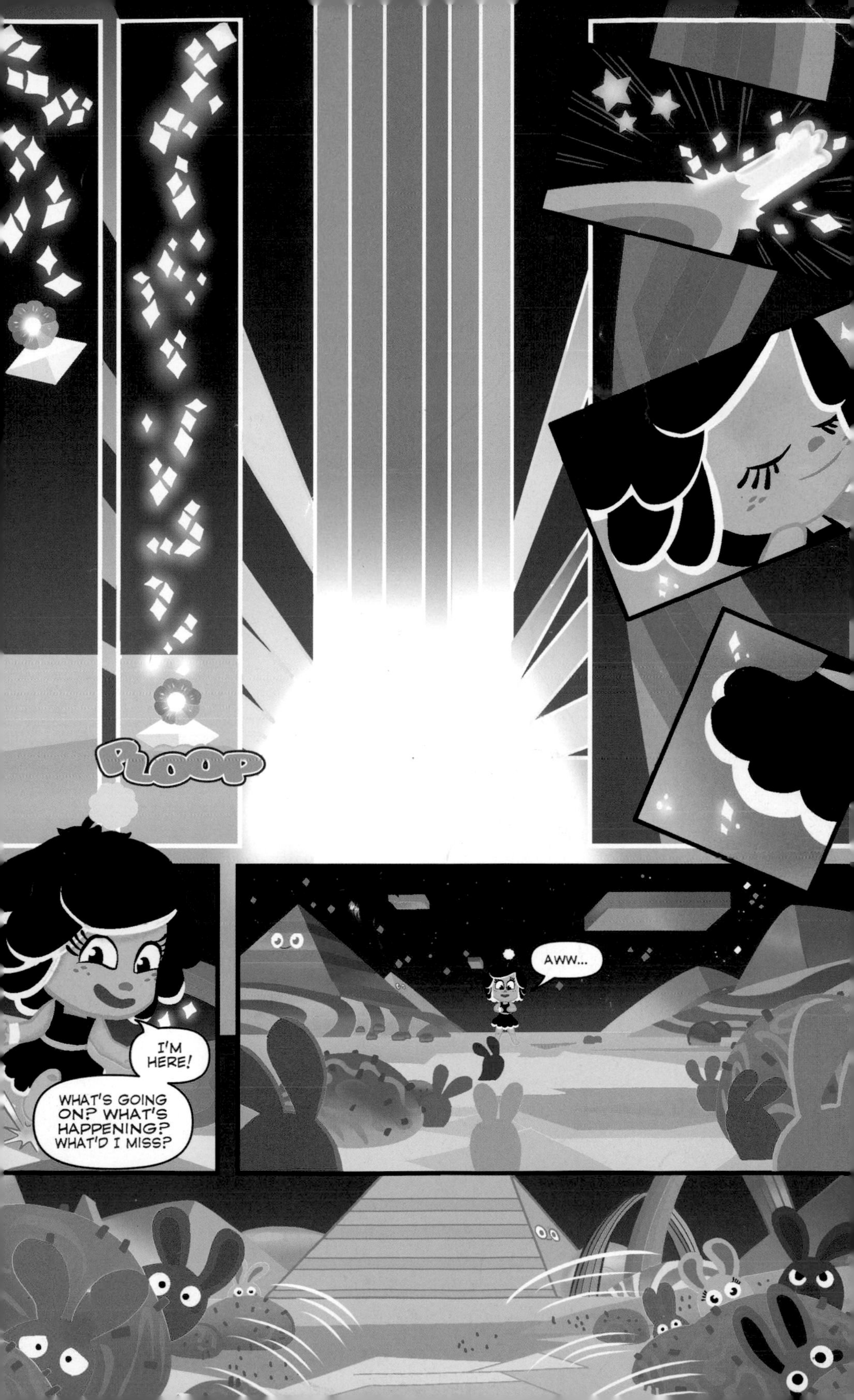
PLOOP
I'M HERE!
WHAT'S GOING ON? WHAT'S HAPPENING? WHAT'D I MISS?
AWW...

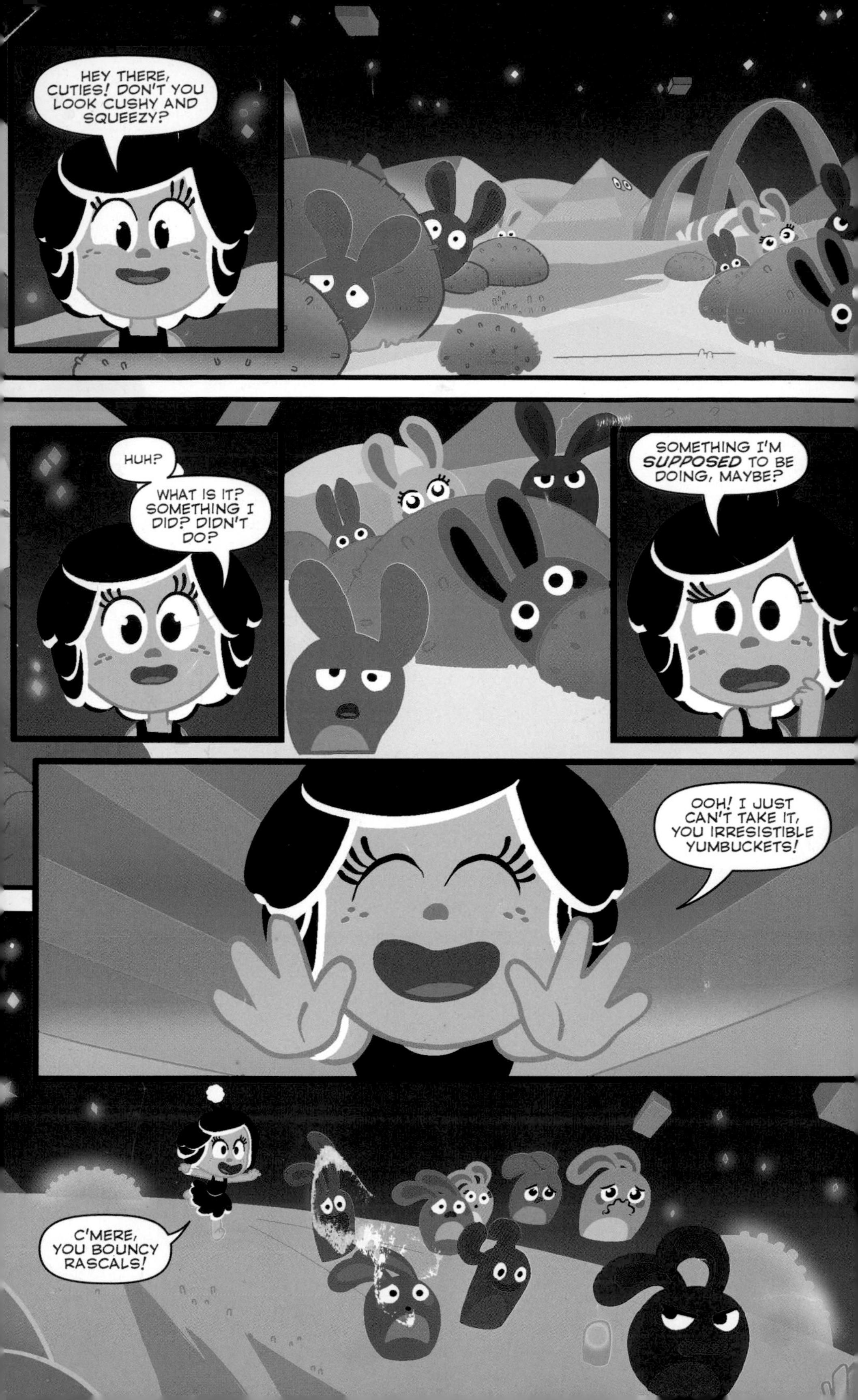

HEY THERE, CUTIES! DON'T YOU LOOK CUSHY AND SQUEEZY?
HUH?
WHAT IS IT? SOMETHING I DID? DIDN'T DO?
SOMETHING I'M *SUPPOSED* TO BE DOING, MAYBE?
OOH! I JUST CAN'T TAKE IT, YOU IRRESISTIBLE YUMBUCKETS!
C'MERE, YOU BOUNCY RASCALS!

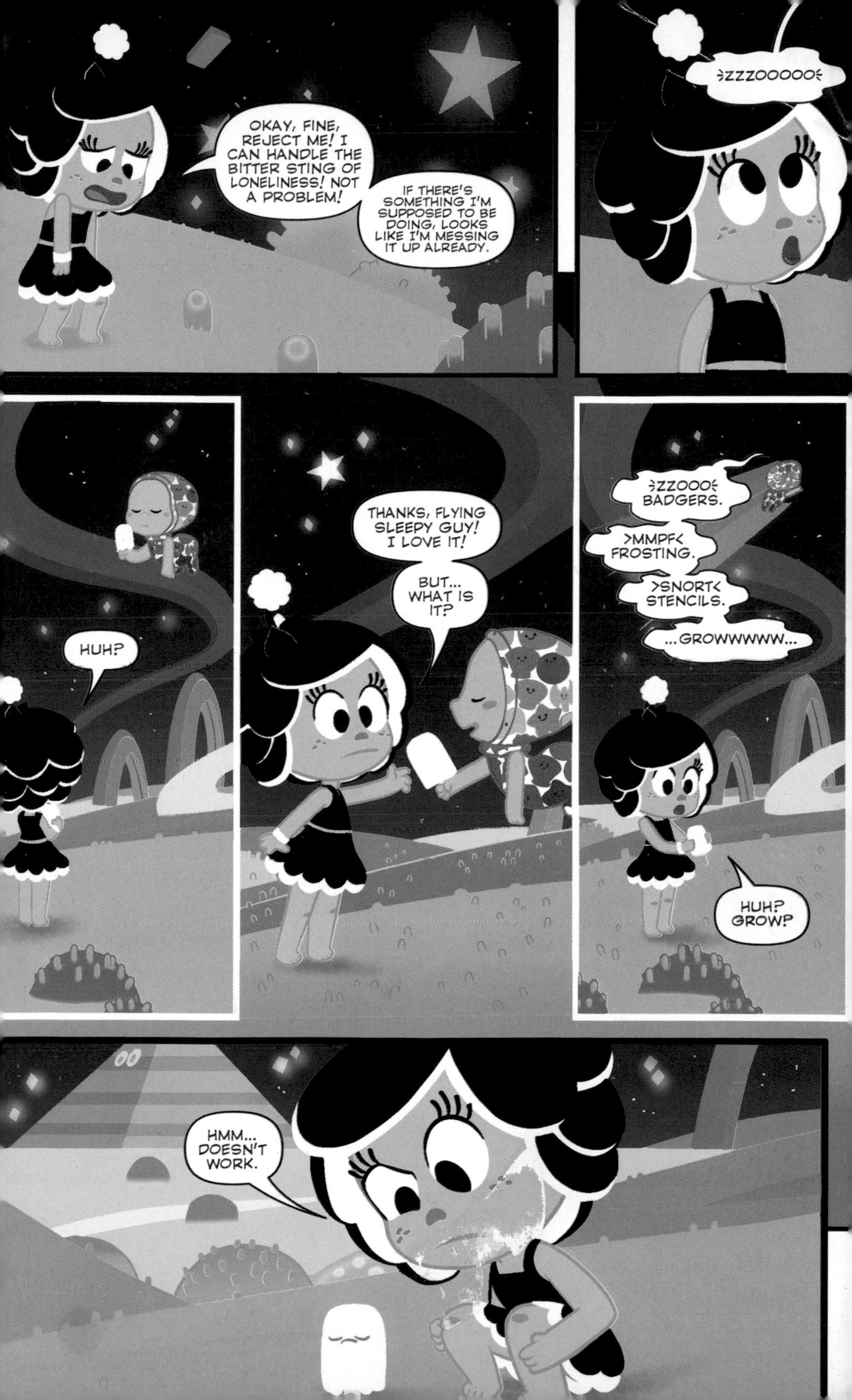
OKAY, FINE, REJECT ME! I CAN HANDLE THE BITTER STING OF LONELINESS! NOT A PROBLEM!
IF THERE'S SOMETHING I'M SUPPOSED TO BE DOING, LOOKS LIKE I'M MESSING IT UP ALREADY.
>ZZZOOOOO<
HUH?
THANKS, FLYING SLEEPY GUY! I LOVE IT!
BUT... WHAT IS IT?
>ZZOOO< BADGERS.
>MMPF< FROSTING.
>SNORT< STENCILS.
...GROWWWWW...
HUH? GROW?
HMM... DOESN'T WORK.

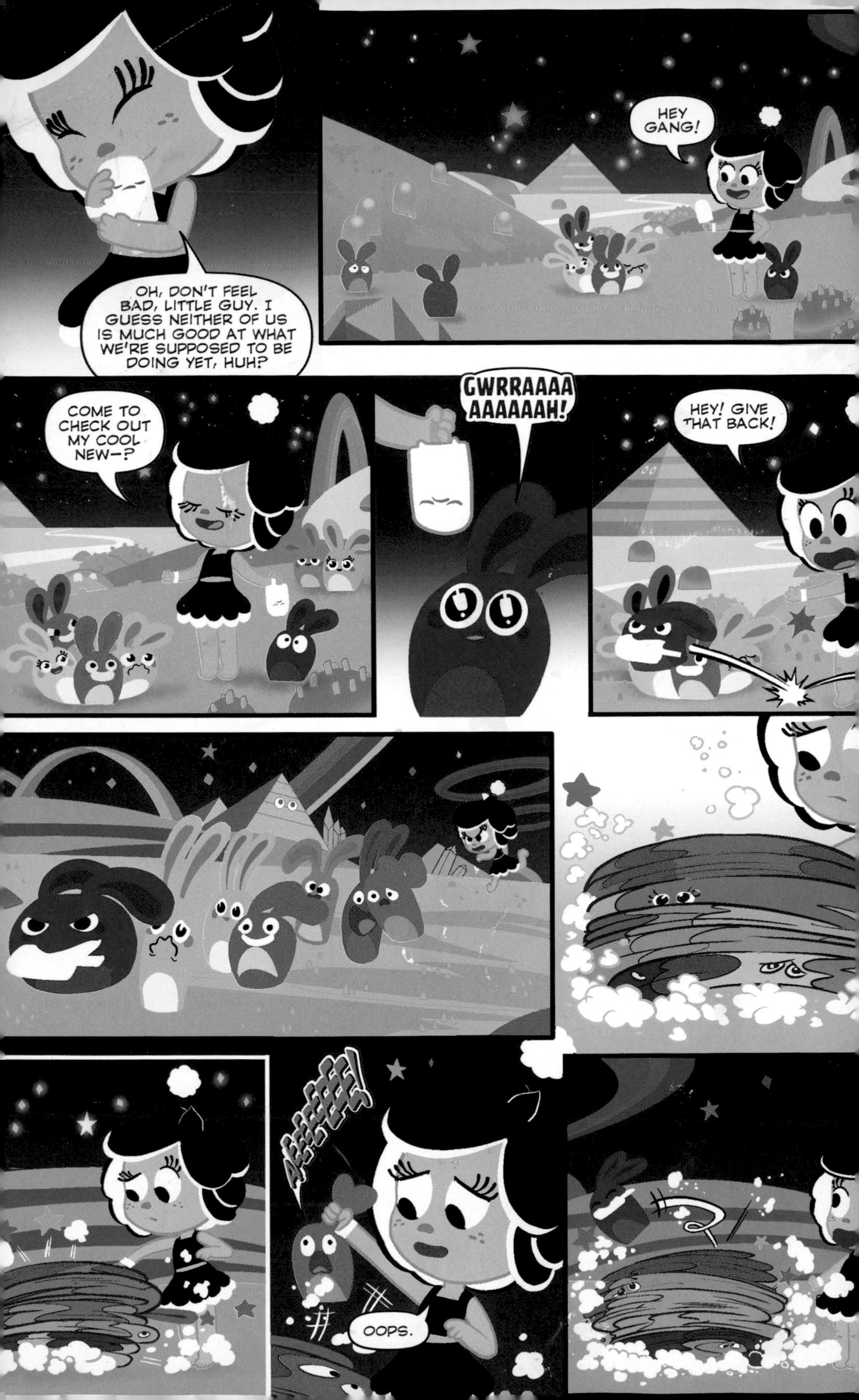
OH, DON'T FEEL BAD, LITTLE GUY. I GUESS NEITHER OF US IS MUCH GOOD AT WHAT WE'RE SUPPOSED TO BE DOING YET, HUH?
HEY GANG!
COME TO CHECK OUT MY COOL NEW-?
GWRRAAAA AAAAAAH!
HEY! GIVE THAT BACK!
OOPS.

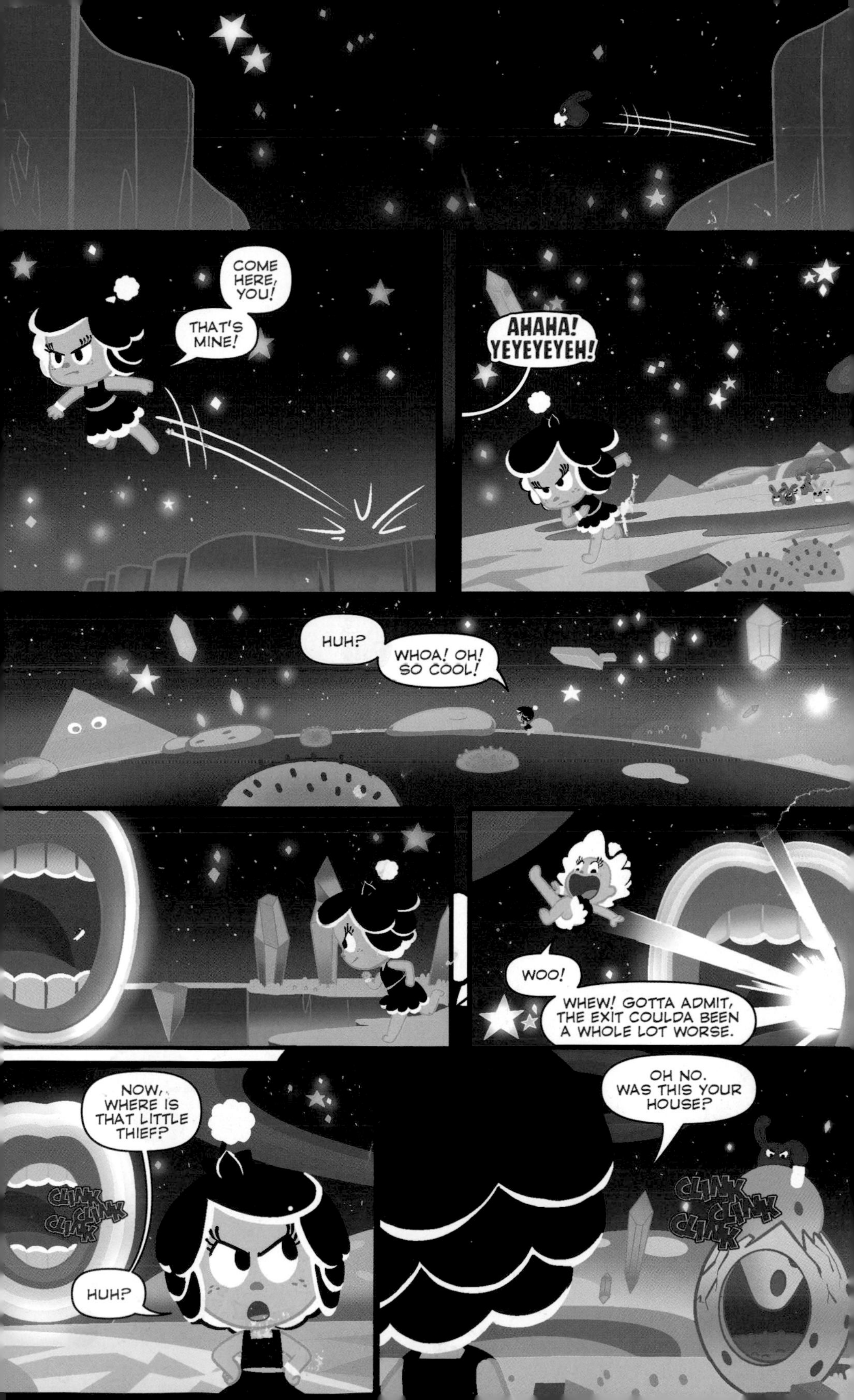
COME HERE, YOU!
THAT'S MINE!
AHAHA! YEYEYEYEH!
HUH?
WHOA! OH! SO COOL!
WOO!
WHEW! GOTTA ADMIT, THE EXIT COULDA BEEN A WHOLE LOT WORSE.
NOW, WHERE IS THAT LITTLE THIEF?
CLINK CLINK CLINK
HUH?
OH NO. WAS THIS YOUR HOUSE?
CLINK CLINK CLINK

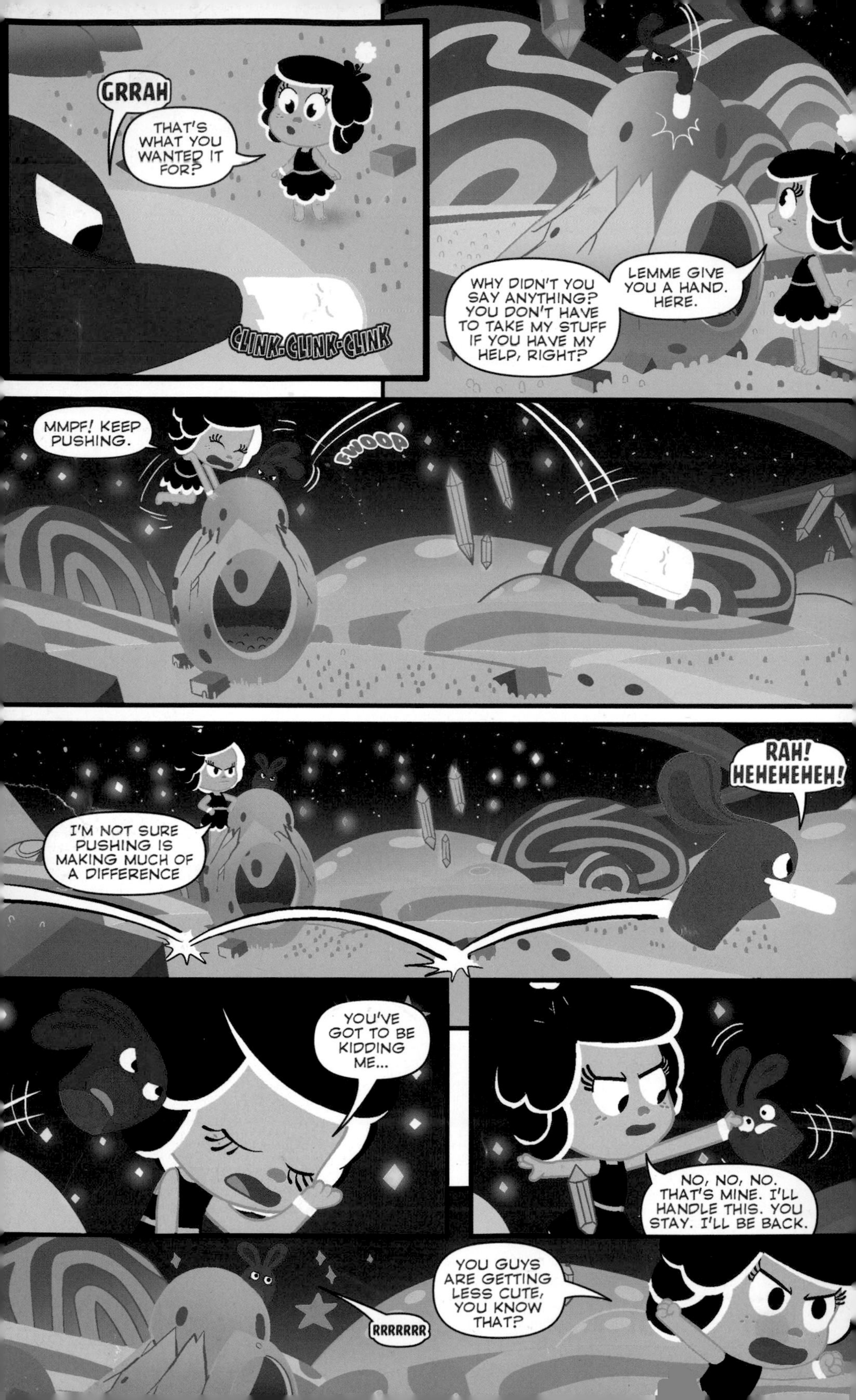
GRRAH
THAT'S WHAT YOU WANTED IT FOR?
CLINK-CLINK-CLINK
WHY DIDN'T YOU SAY ANYTHING? YOU DON'T HAVE TO TAKE MY STUFF IF YOU HAVE MY HELP, RIGHT?
LEMME GIVE YOU A HAND. HERE.
MMPF! KEEP PUSHING.
FWOOP
I'M NOT SURE PUSHING IS MAKING MUCH OF A DIFFERENCE
RAH! HEHEHEHEH!
YOU'VE GOT TO BE KIDDING ME...
NO, NO, NO. THAT'S MINE. I'LL HANDLE THIS. YOU STAY. I'LL BE BACK.
RRRRRRR
YOU GUYS ARE GETTING LESS CUTE, YOU KNOW THAT?

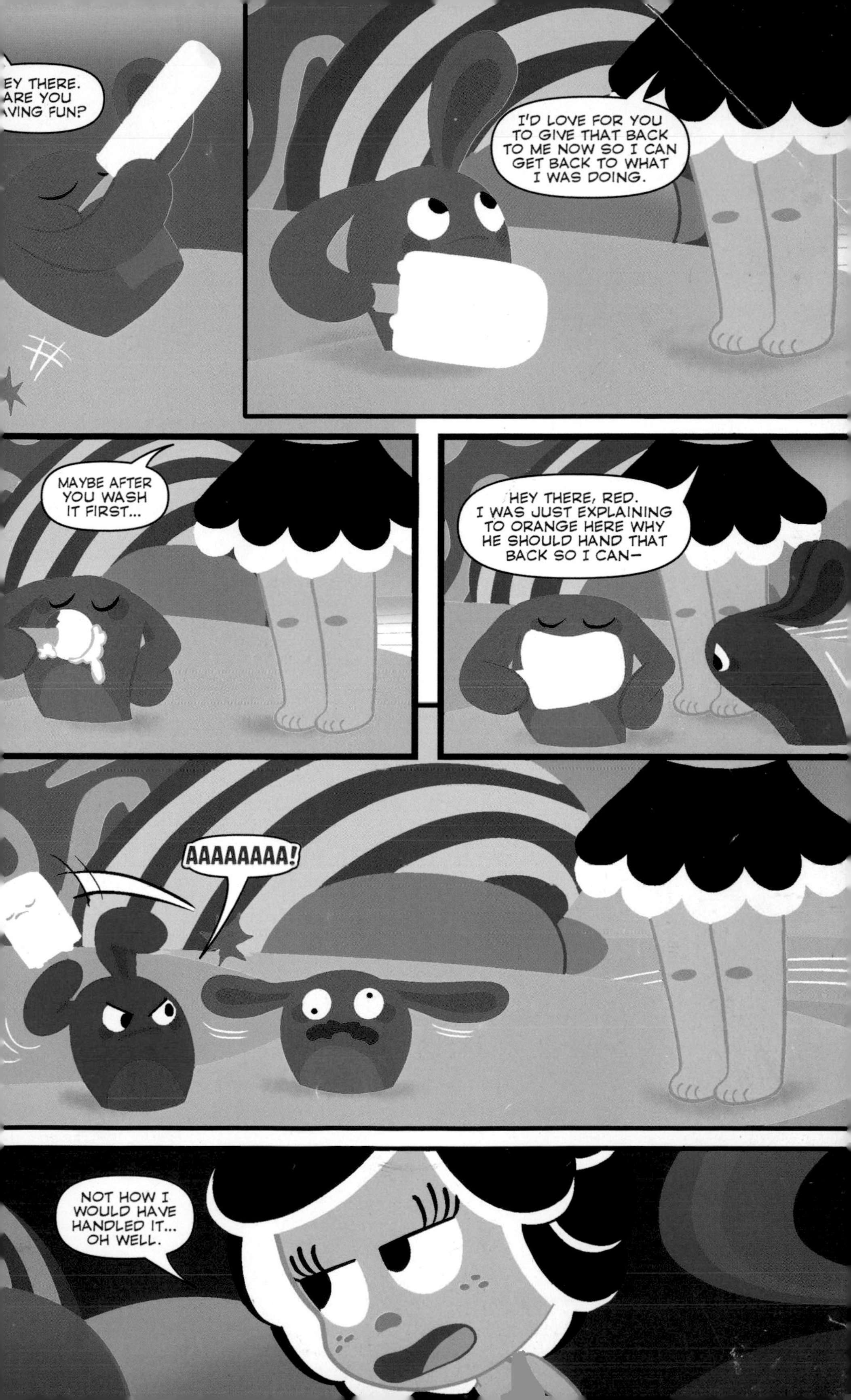
EY THERE.
ARE YOU
AVING FUN?
I'D LOVE FOR YOU TO GIVE THAT BACK TO ME NOW SO I CAN GET BACK TO WHAT I WAS DOING.
MAYBE AFTER YOU WASH IT FIRST...
HEY THERE, RED. I WAS JUST EXPLAINING TO ORANGE HERE WHY HE SHOULD HAND THAT BACK SO I CAN—
AAAAAAAA!
NOT HOW I WOULD HAVE HANDLED IT... OH WELL.

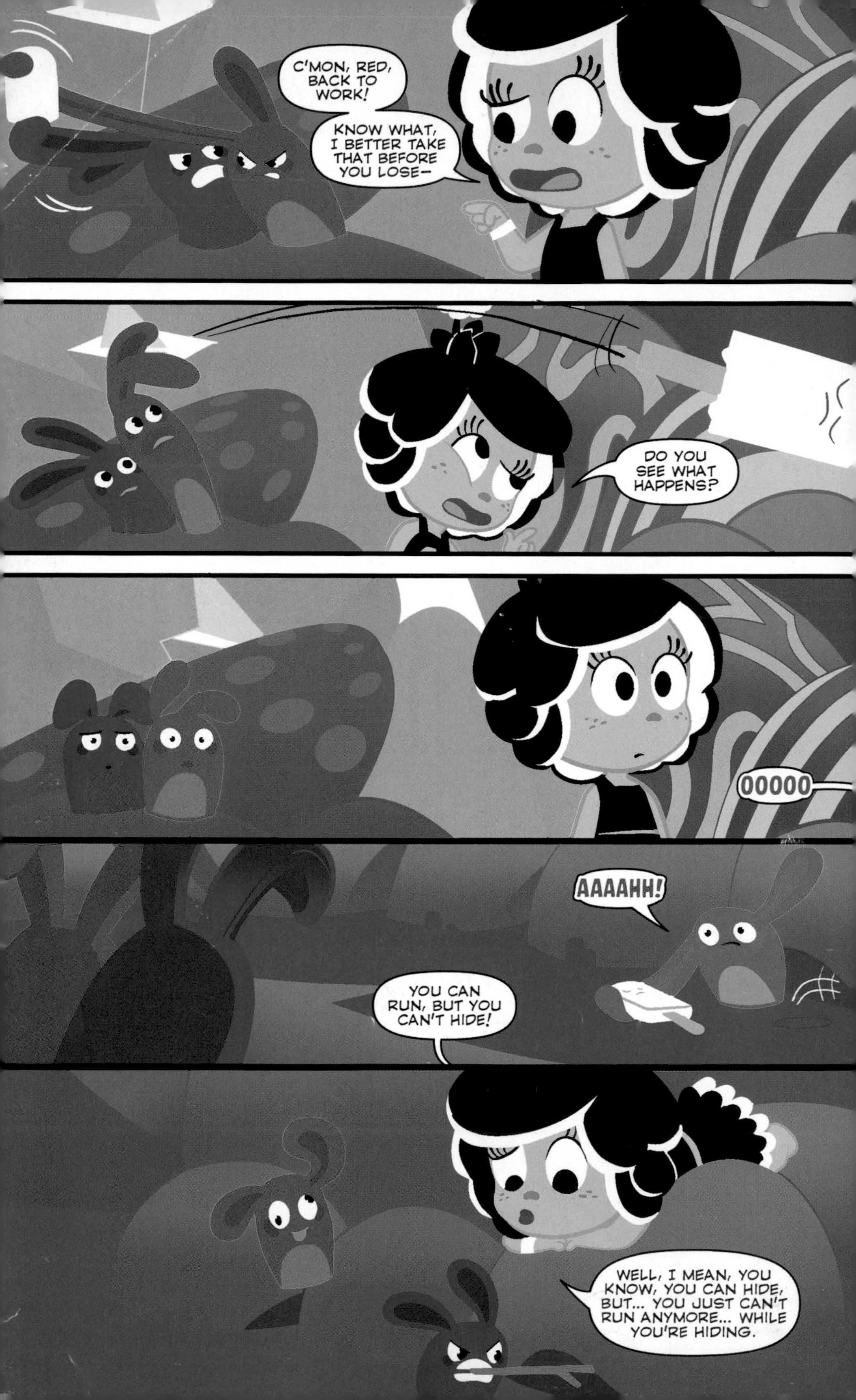
C'MON, RED, BACK TO WORK!
KNOW WHAT, I BETTER TAKE THAT BEFORE YOU LOSE—
DO YOU SEE WHAT HAPPENS?
OOOOO
AAAAHH!
YOU CAN RUN, BUT YOU CAN'T HIDE!
WELL, I MEAN, YOU KNOW, YOU CAN HIDE, BUT... YOU JUST CAN'T RUN ANYMORE... WHILE YOU'RE HIDING.

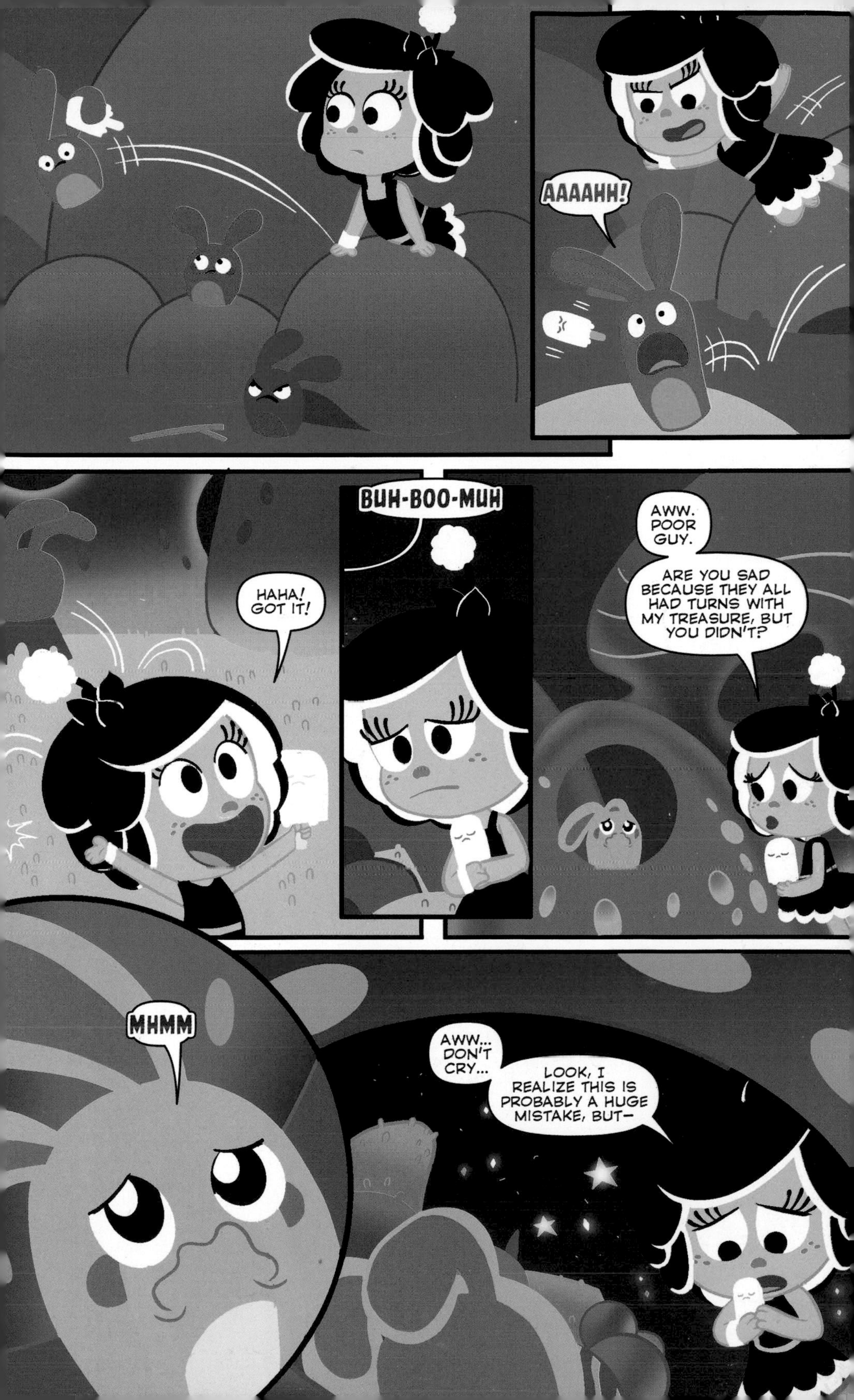
AAAAHH!
HAHA! GOT IT!
BUH-BOO-MUH
AWW. POOR GUY.
ARE YOU SAD BECAUSE THEY ALL HAD TURNS WITH MY TREASURE, BUT YOU DIDN'T?
MHMM
AWW... DON'T CRY...
LOOK, I REALIZE THIS IS PROBABLY A HUGE MISTAKE, BUT–

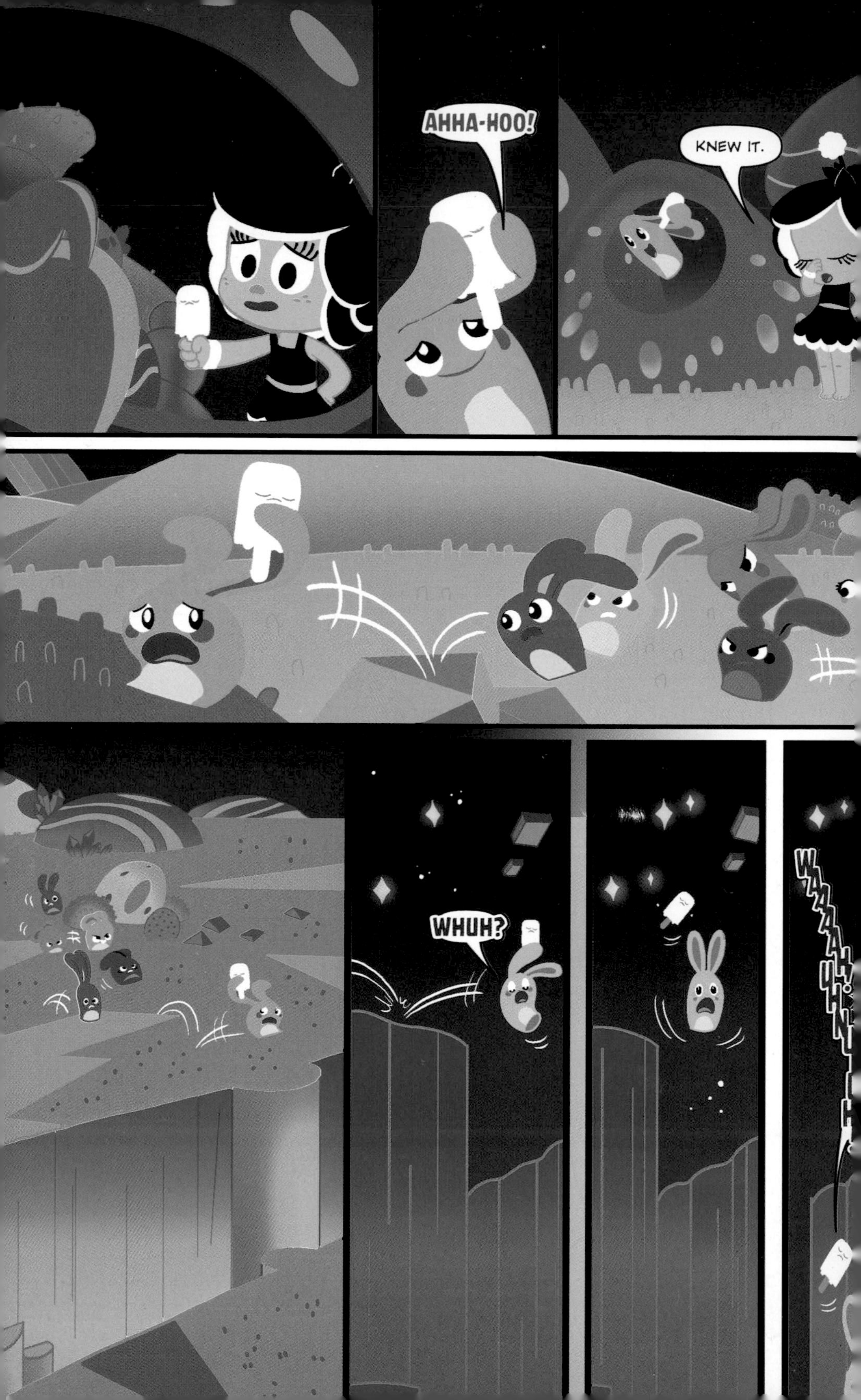
AHHA-HOO!
KNEW IT.
WHUH?

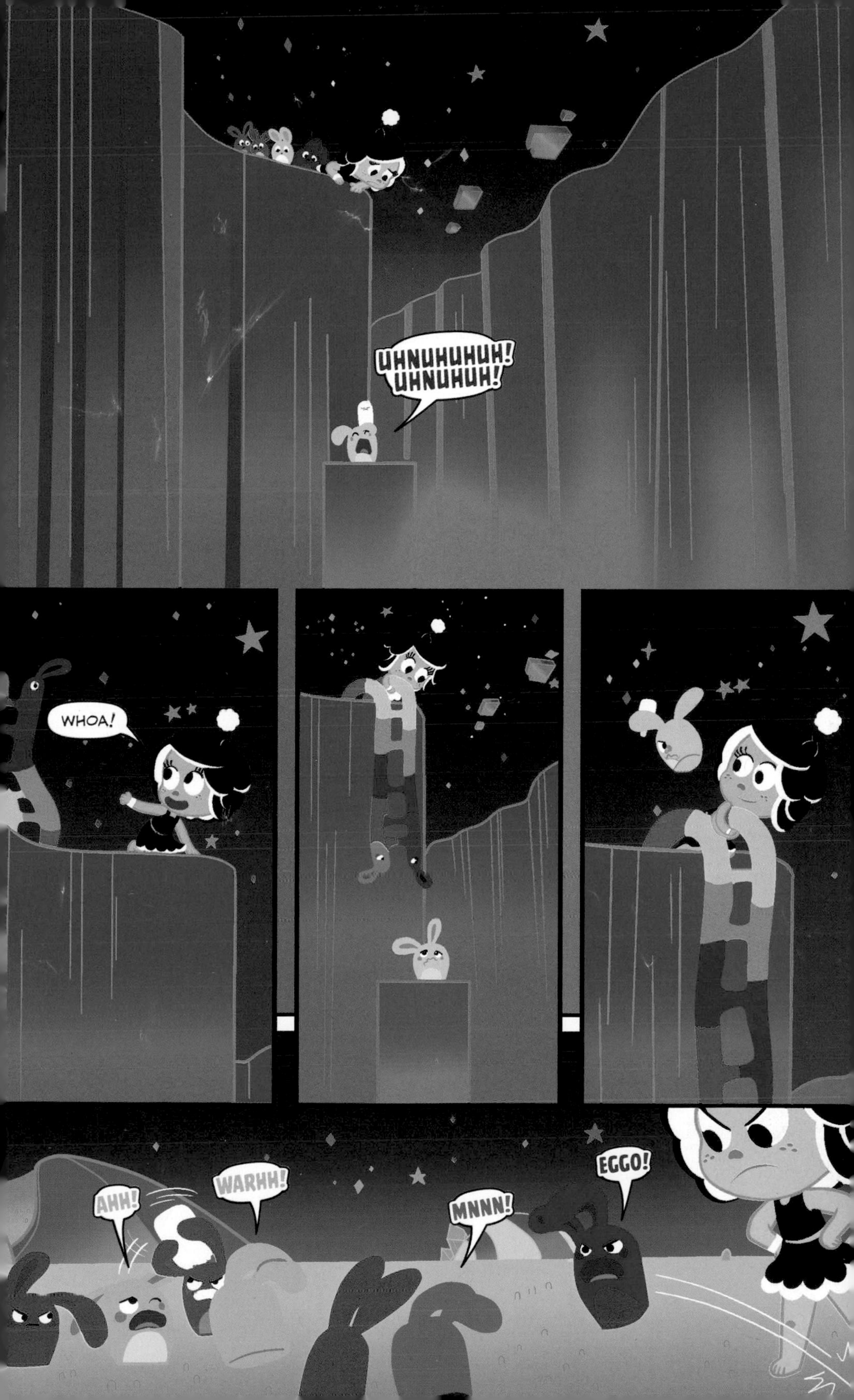
UHNUHUHUH! UHNUHUH!
WHOA!
AHH!
WARHH!
MNNN!
EGGO!

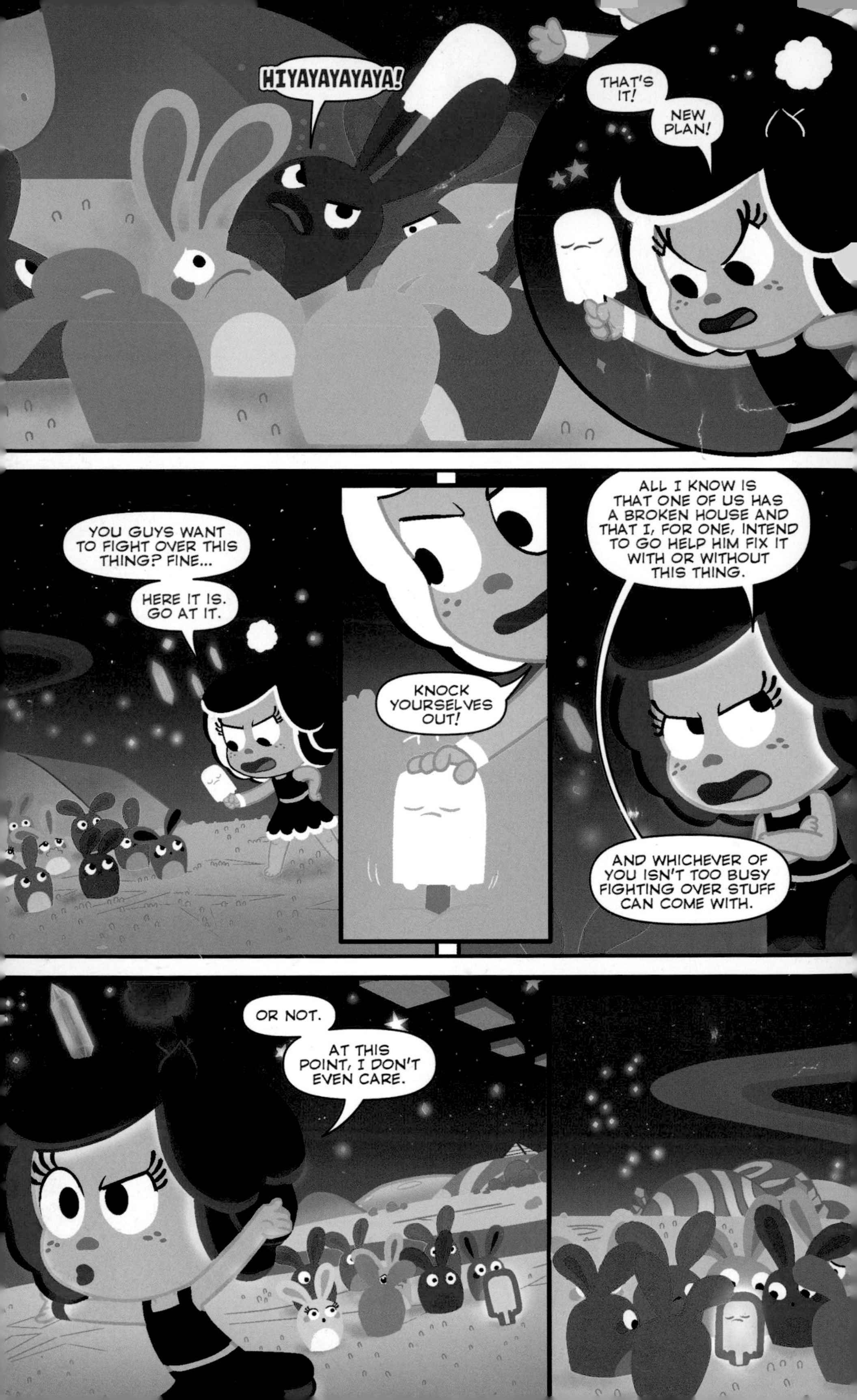
HIYAYAYAYAYA!
THAT'S IT!
NEW PLAN!
YOU GUYS WANT TO FIGHT OVER THIS THING? FINE...
HERE IT IS. GO AT IT.
KNOCK YOURSELVES OUT!
ALL I KNOW IS THAT ONE OF US HAS A BROKEN HOUSE AND THAT I, FOR ONE, INTEND TO GO HELP HIM FIX IT WITH OR WITHOUT THIS THING.
AND WHICHEVER OF YOU ISN'T TOO BUSY FIGHTING OVER STUFF CAN COME WITH.
OR NOT.
AT THIS POINT, I DON'T EVEN CARE.

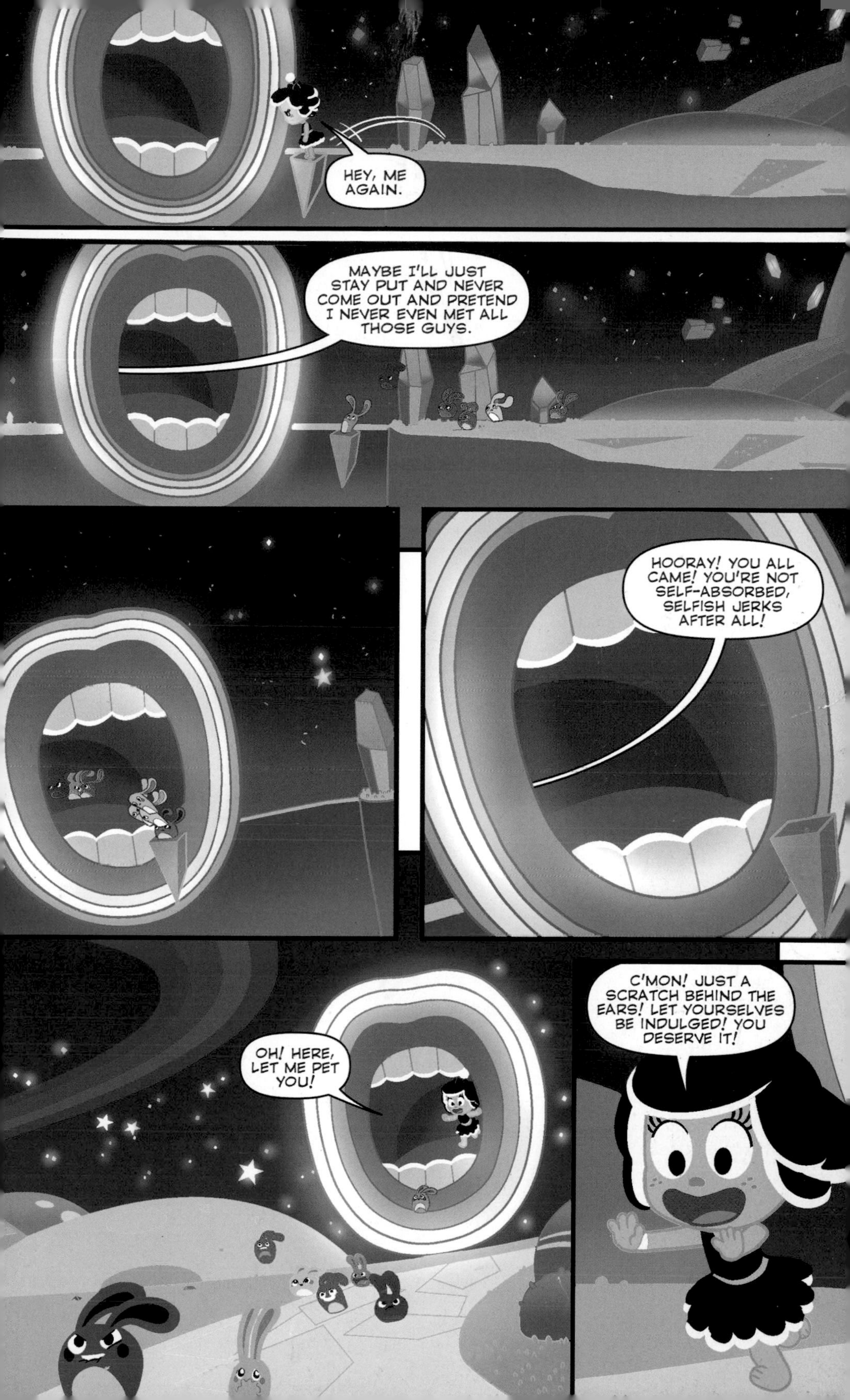
HEY, ME AGAIN.
MAYBE I'LL JUST STAY PUT AND NEVER COME OUT AND PRETEND I NEVER EVEN MET ALL THOSE GUYS.
HOORAY! YOU ALL CAME! YOU'RE NOT SELF-ABSORBED, SELFISH JERKS AFTER ALL!
OH! HERE, LET ME PET YOU!
C'MON! JUST A SCRATCH BEHIND THE EARS! LET YOURSELVES BE INDULGED! YOU DESERVE IT!

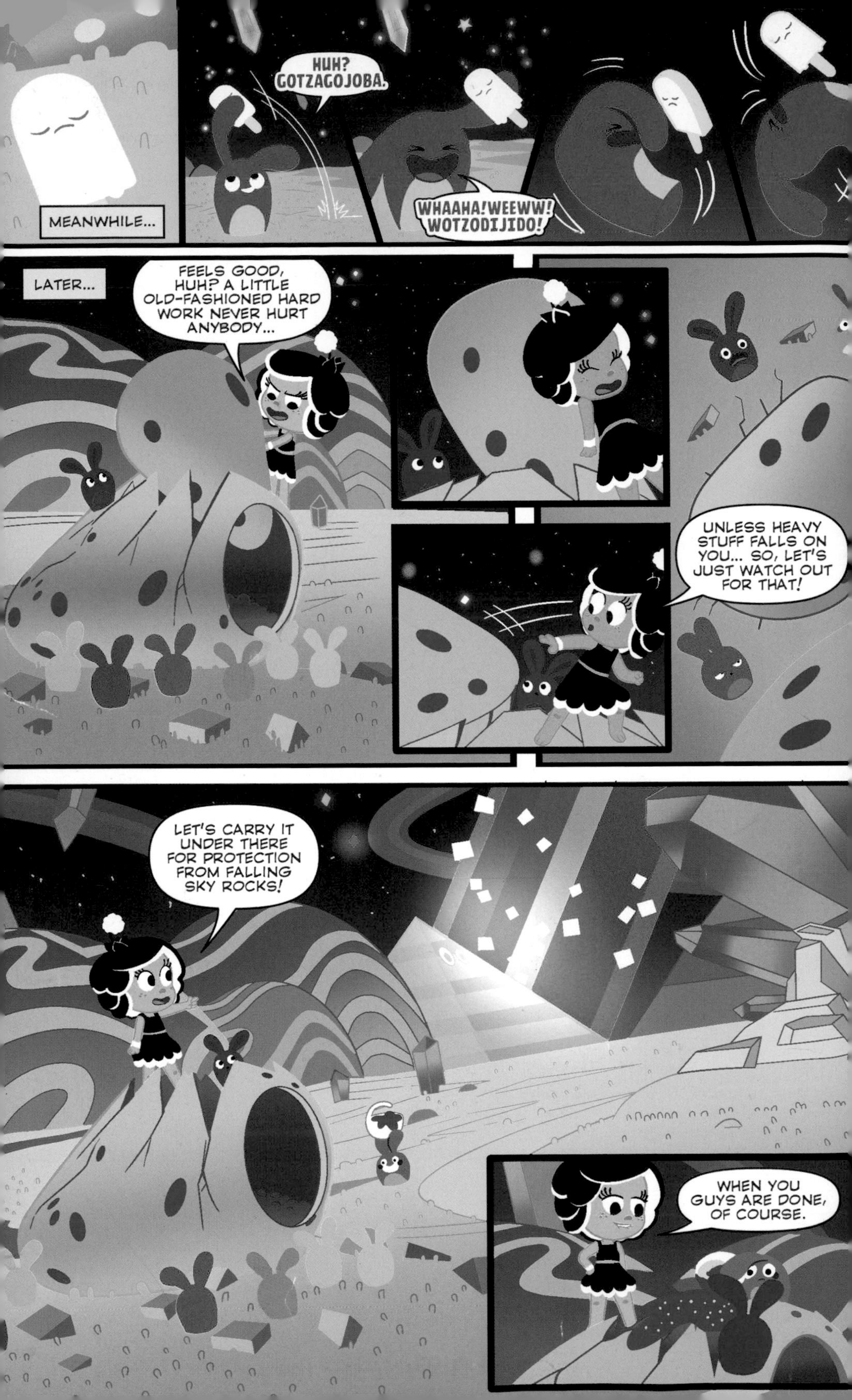
MEANWHILE...
HUH? GOTZAGOJOBA.
WHAAHA! WEEWW! WOTZODIJIDO!
LATER...
FEELS GOOD, HUH? A LITTLE OLD-FASHIONED HARD WORK NEVER HURT ANYBODY...
UNLESS HEAVY STUFF FALLS ON YOU... SO, LET'S JUST WATCH OUT FOR THAT!
LET'S CARRY IT UNDER THERE FOR PROTECTION FROM FALLING SKY ROCKS!
WHEN YOU GUYS ARE DONE, OF COURSE.

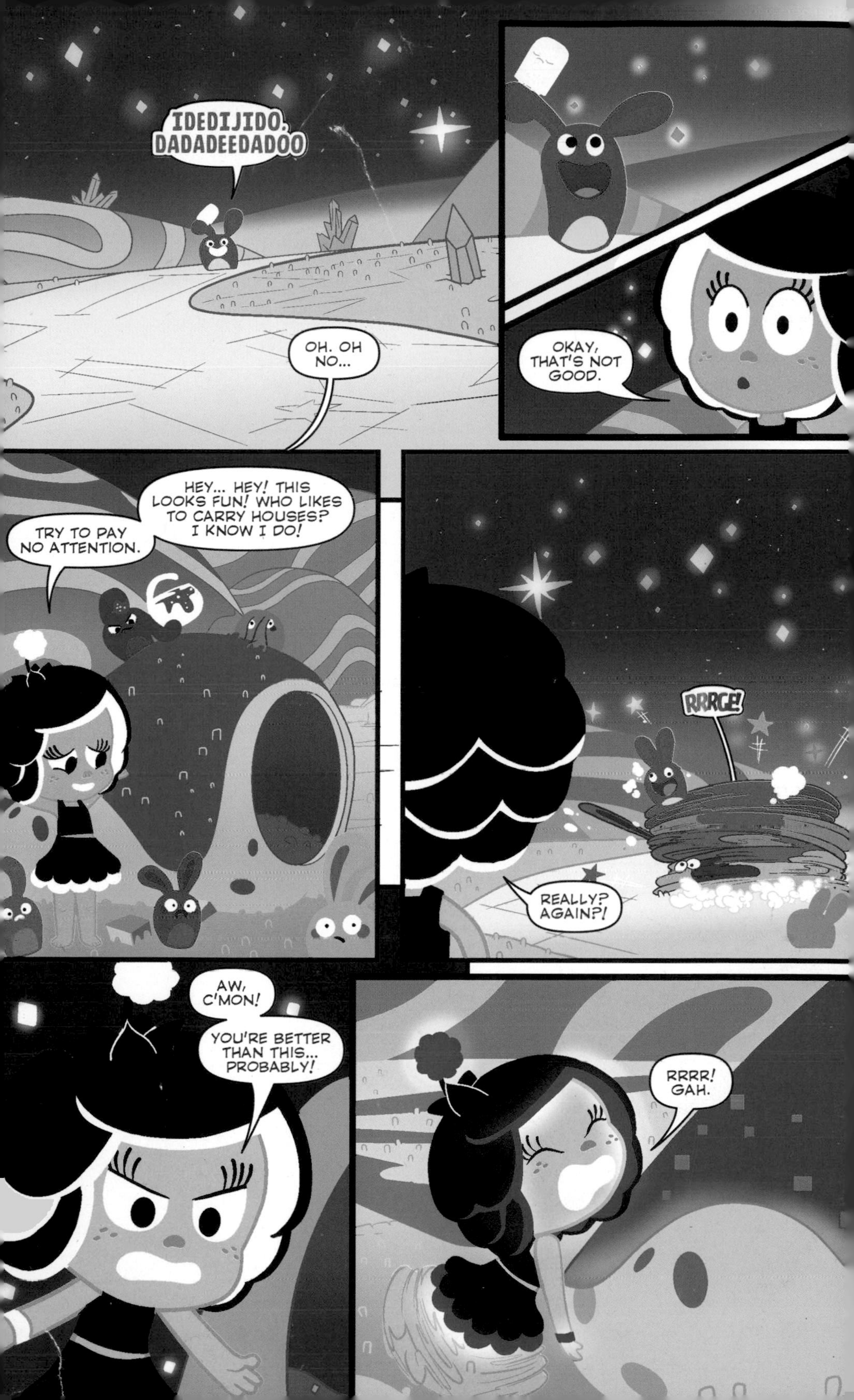
IDEDIJIDO, DADADEEDADOO
OH. OH NO...
OKAY, THAT'S NOT GOOD.
TRY TO PAY NO ATTENTION.
HEY... HEY! THIS LOOKS FUN! WHO LIKES TO CARRY HOUSES? I KNOW I DO!
RRRGE!
REALLY? AGAIN?!
AW, C'MON!
YOU'RE BETTER THAN THIS... PROBABLY!
RRRR! GAH.

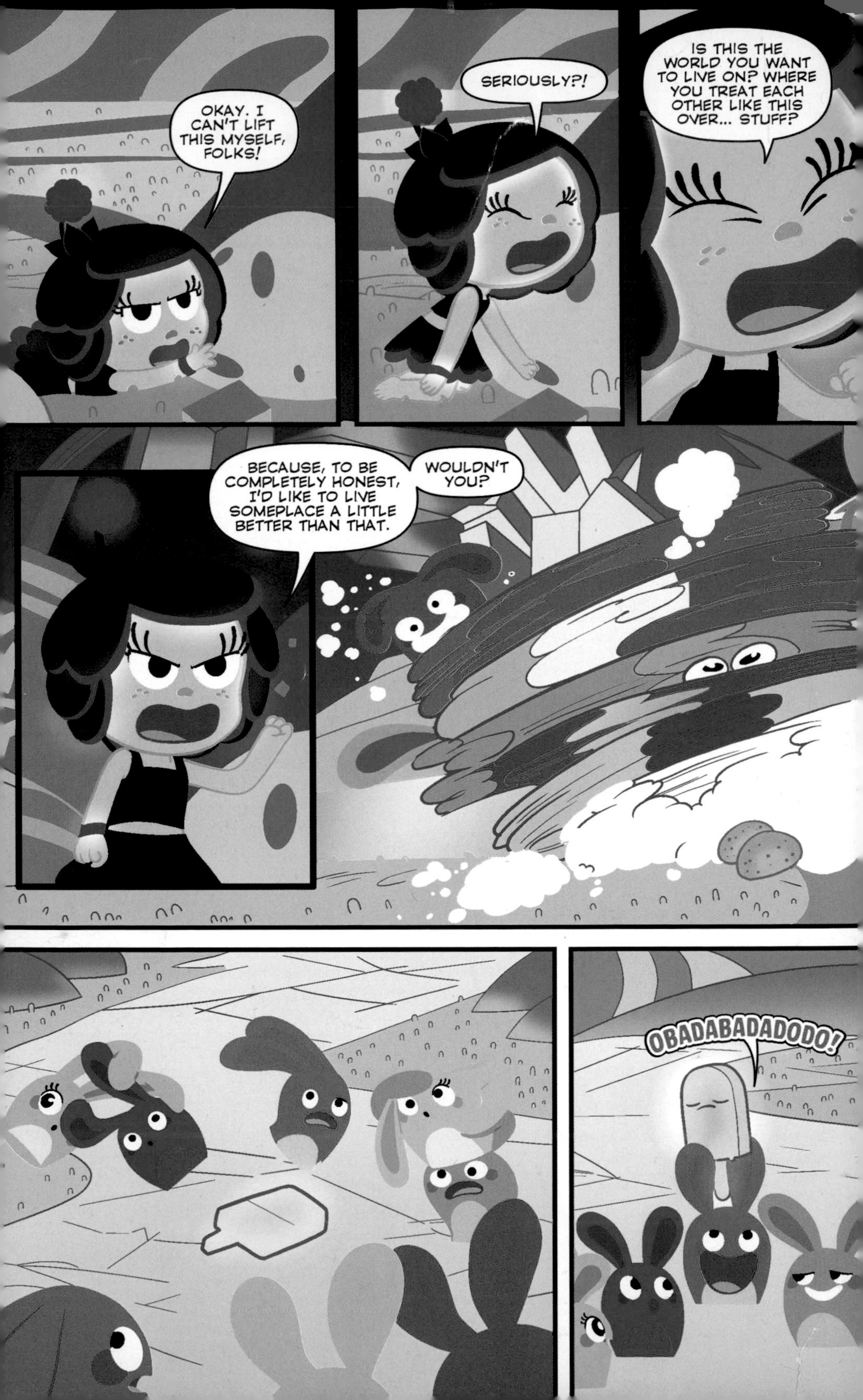
OKAY. I CAN'T LIFT THIS MYSELF, FOLKS!
SERIOUSLY?!
IS THIS THE WORLD YOU WANT TO LIVE ON? WHERE YOU TREAT EACH OTHER LIKE THIS OVER... STUFF?
BECAUSE, TO BE COMPLETELY HONEST, I'D LIKE TO LIVE SOMEPLACE A LITTLE BETTER THAN THAT.
WOULDN'T YOU?
OBADABADADODO!

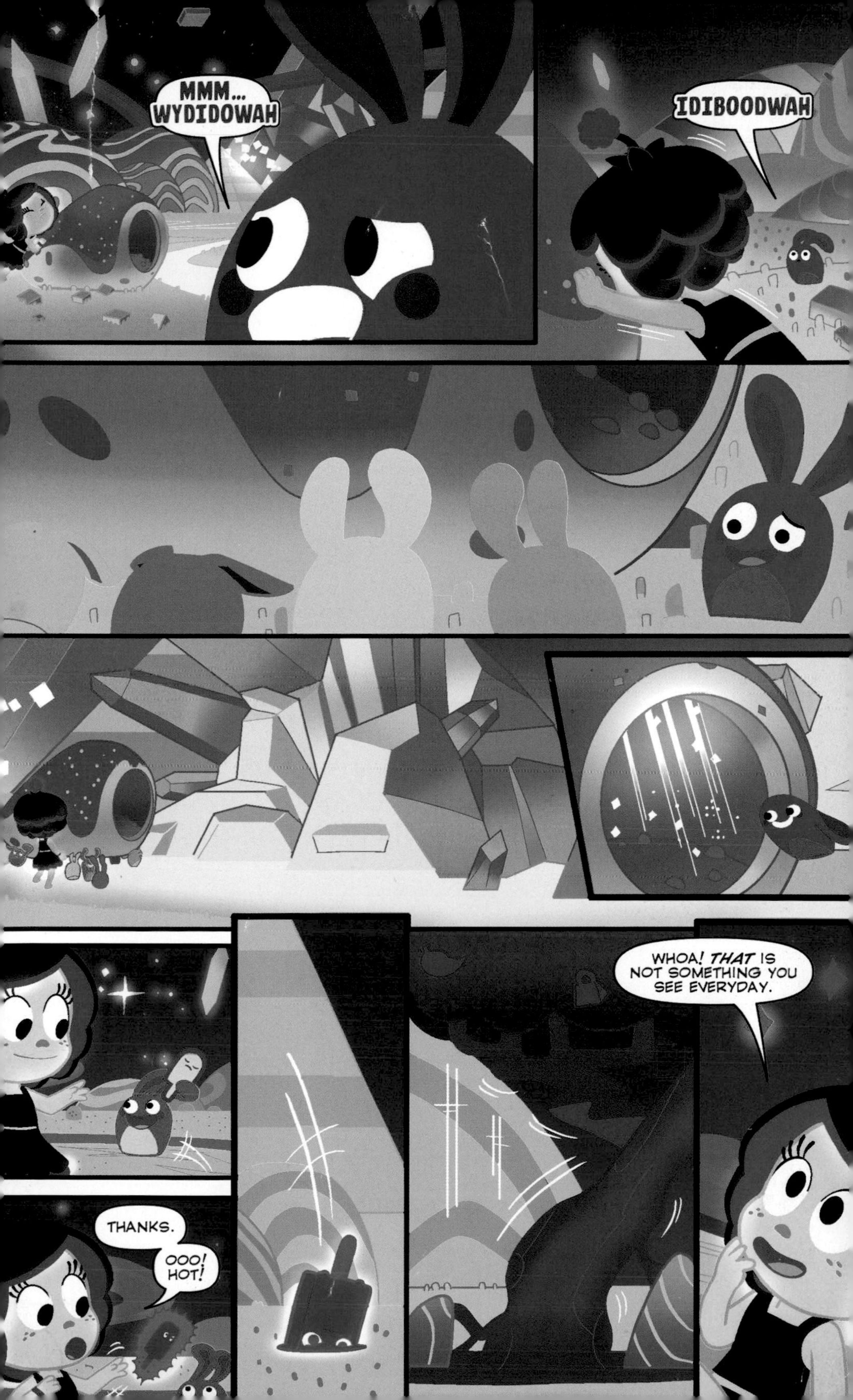
MMM... WYDIDOWAH
IDIBOODWAH
WHOA! THAT IS NOT SOMETHING YOU SEE EVERYDAY.
THANKS.
OOO! HOT!

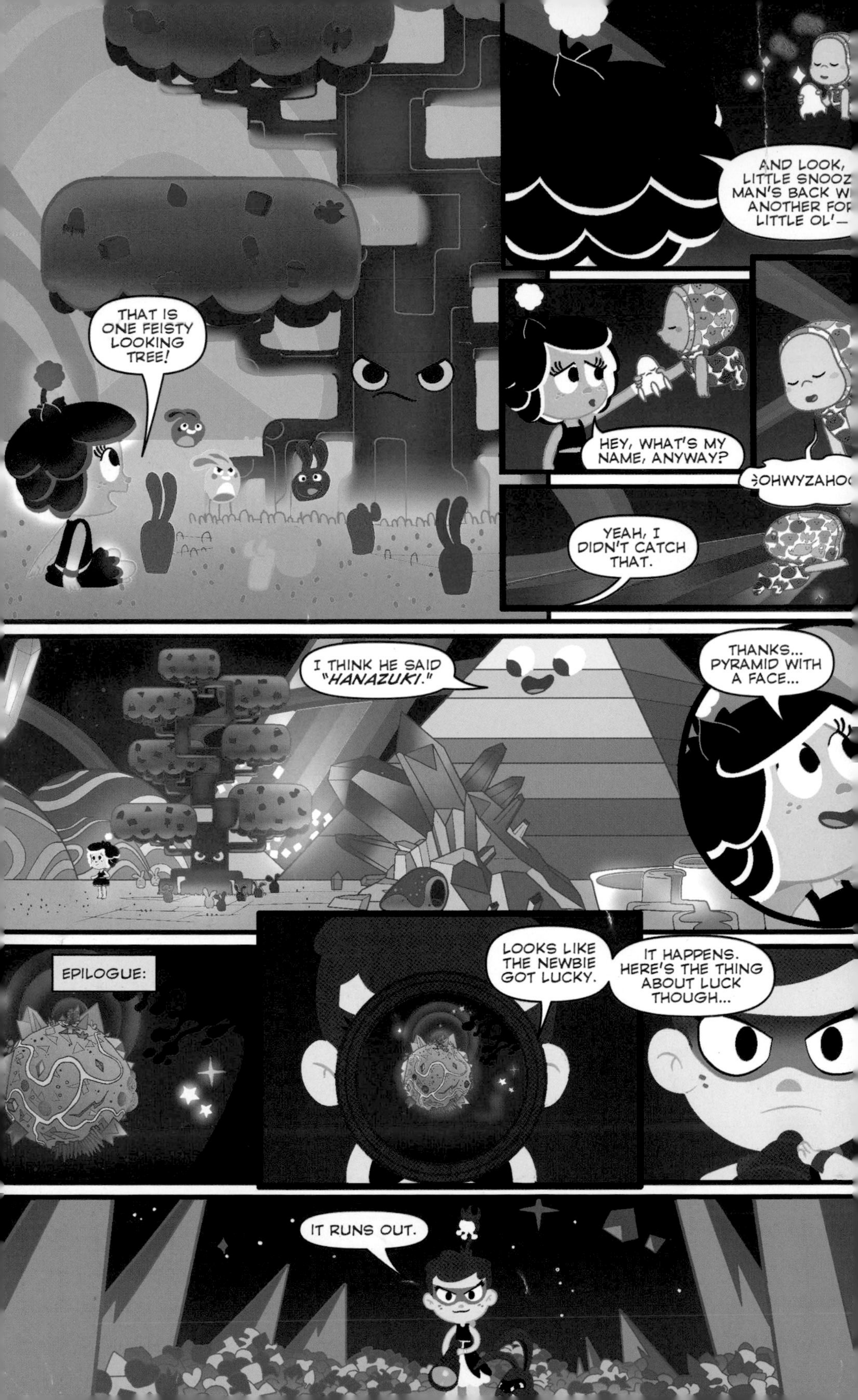
THAT IS ONE FEISTY LOOKING TREE!
AND LOOK, LITTLE SNOOZ MAN'S BACK WI ANOTHER FOR LITTLE OL'—
HEY, WHAT'S MY NAME, ANYWAY?
OHWYZAHO
YEAH, I DIDN'T CATCH THAT.
I THINK HE SAID "*HANAZUKI*."
THANKS... PYRAMID WITH A FACE...
EPILOGUE:
LOOKS LIKE THE NEWBIE GOT LUCKY.
IT HAPPENS. HERE'S THE THING ABOUT LUCK THOUGH...
IT RUNS OUT.

COVER ART BY **YASMIN SHIEKH**

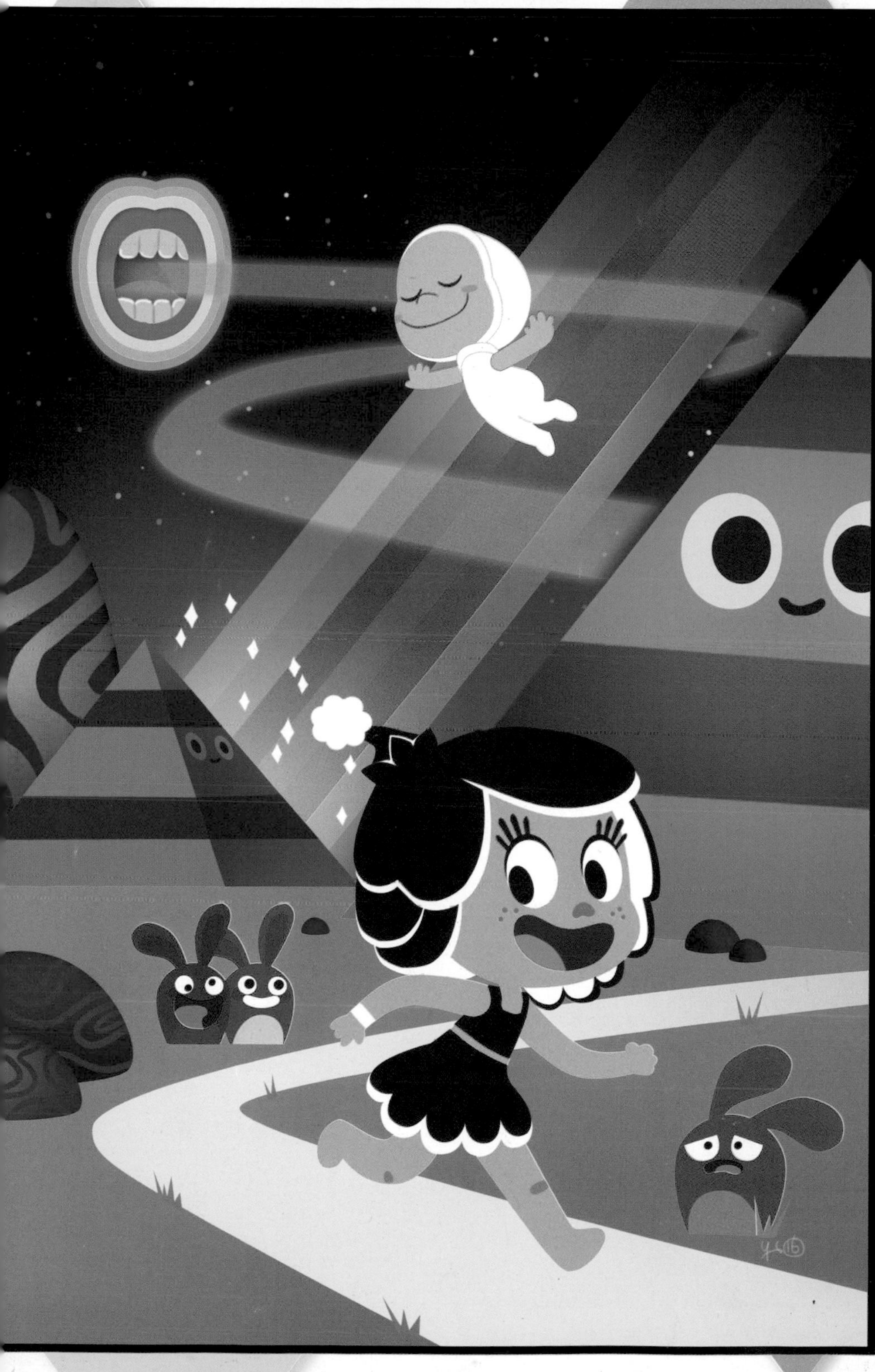

COVER ART BY **NICO PEÑA** COLORS BY **VALENTINA PINTO**

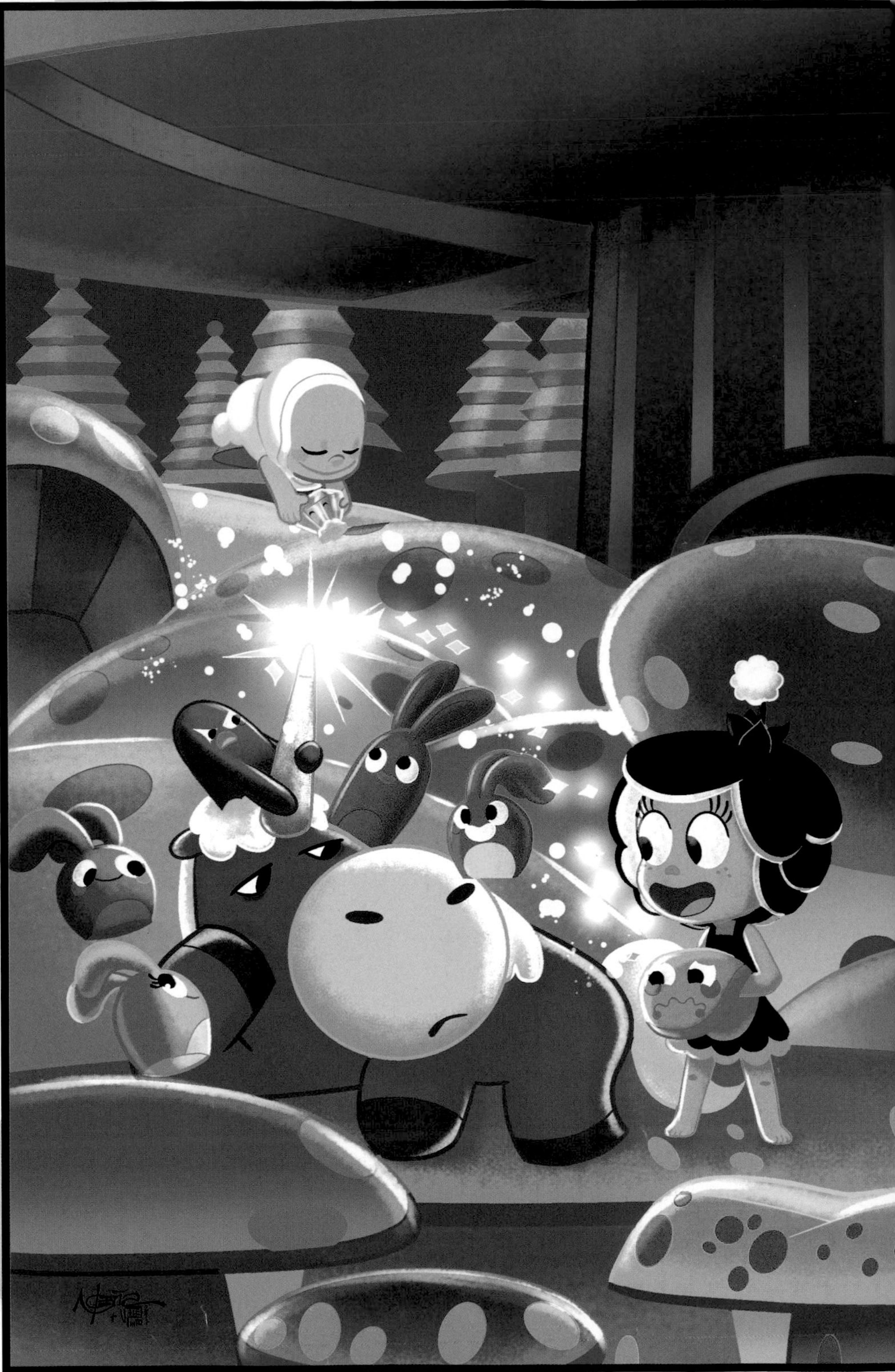

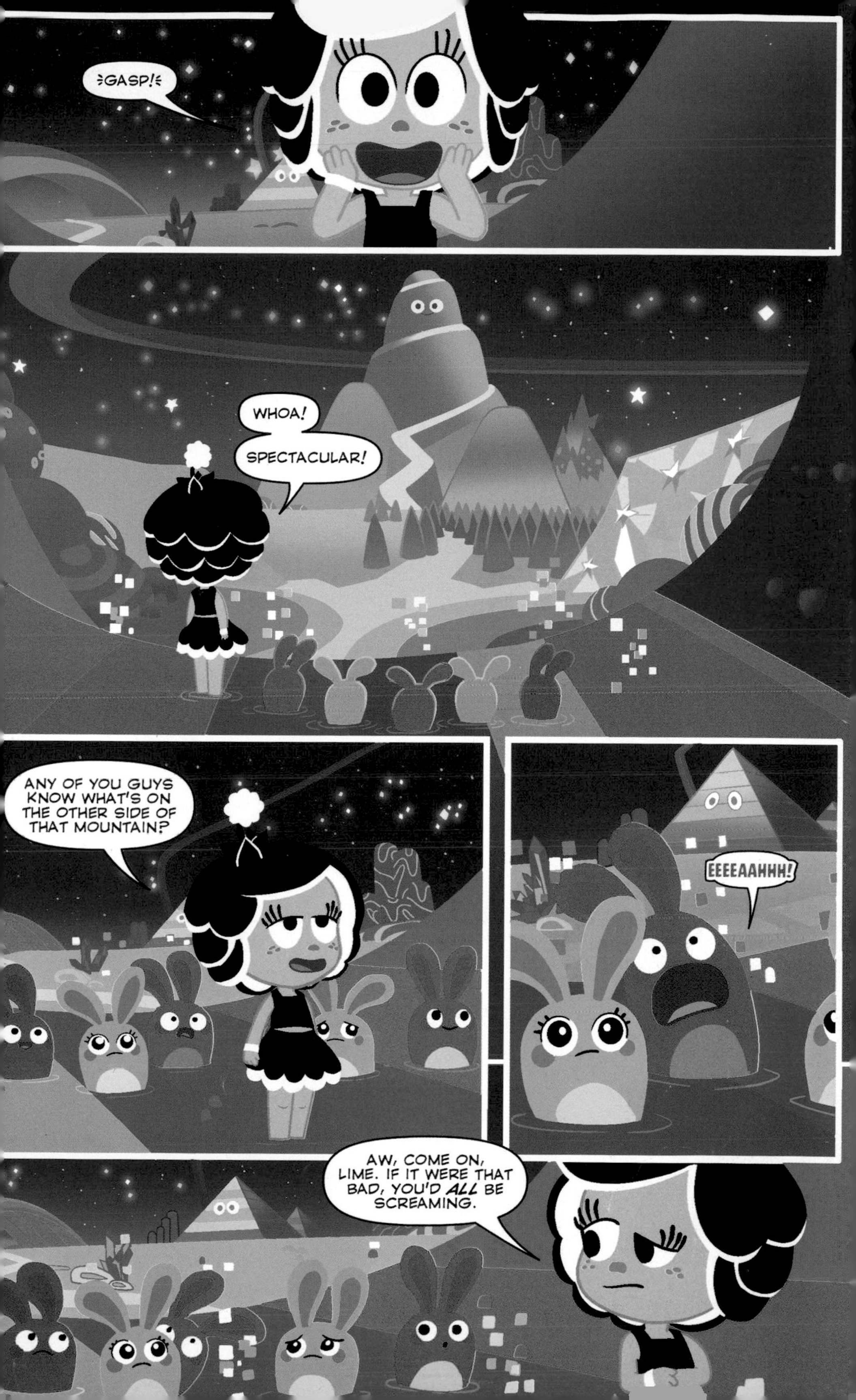
GASP!
WHOA!
SPECTACULAR!
ANY OF YOU GUYS KNOW WHAT'S ON THE OTHER SIDE OF THAT MOUNTAIN?
EEEEAAHHH!
AW, COME ON, LIME. IF IT WERE THAT BAD, YOU'D ALL BE SCREAMING.

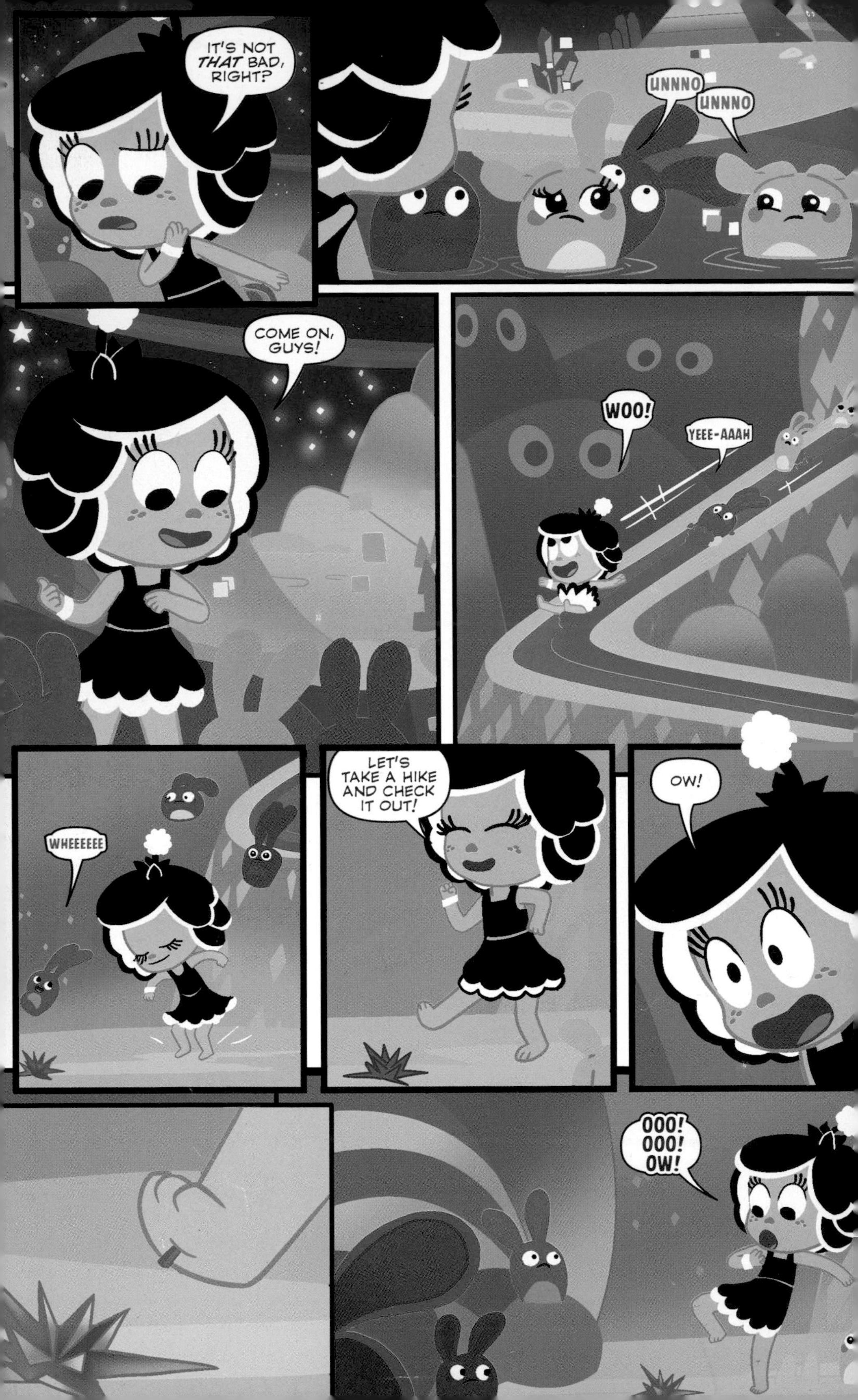
IT'S NOT *THAT* BAD, RIGHT?
UNNNO
UNNNO
COME ON, GUYS!
WOO!
YEEE-AAAH
WHEEEEEE
LET'S TAKE A HIKE AND CHECK IT OUT!
OW!
OOO! OOO! OW!

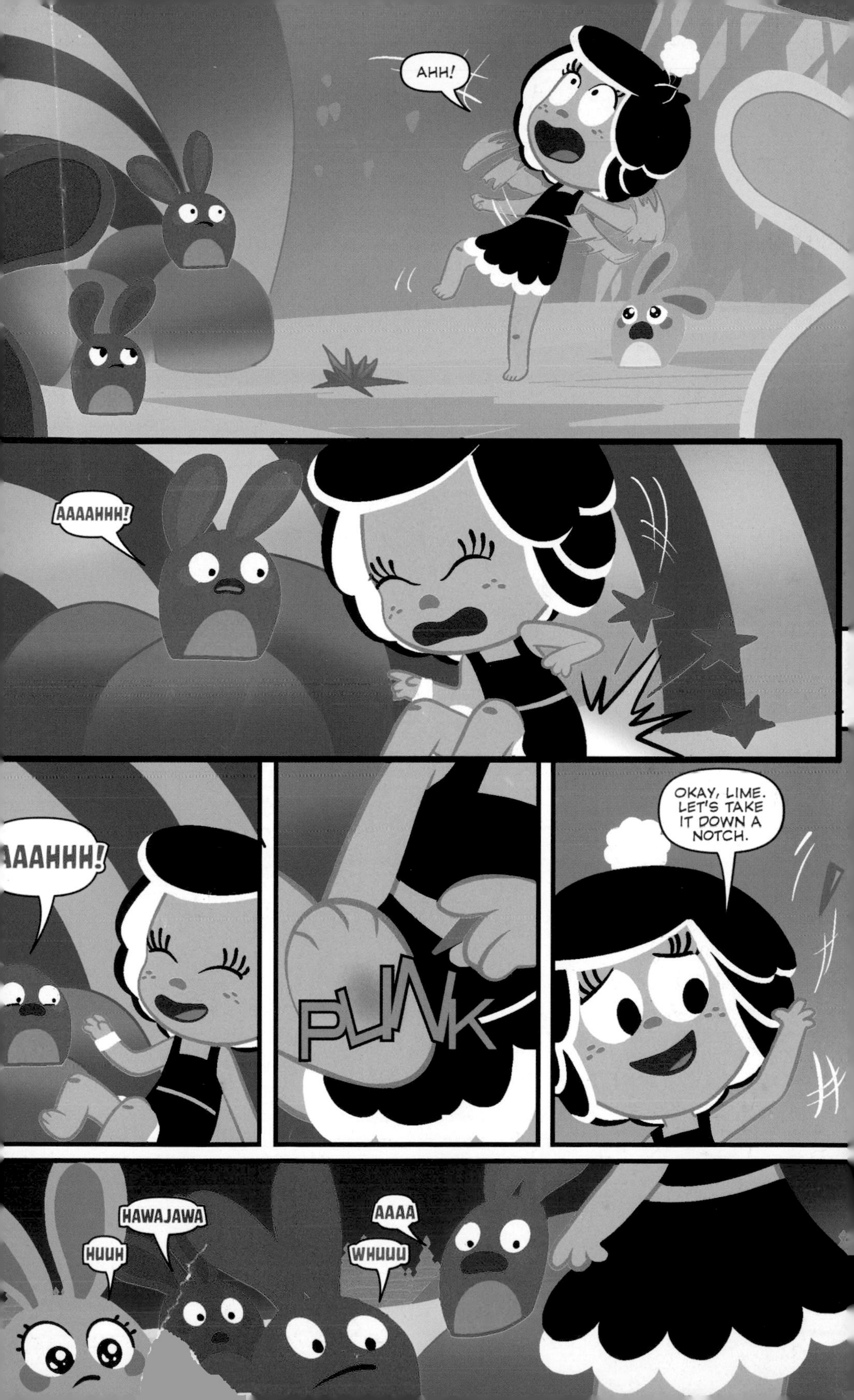
AHH!
AAAAHHH!
AAAHHH!
PLINK
OKAY, LIME. LET'S TAKE IT DOWN A NOTCH.
HAWAJAWA
HUUH
AAAA
WHUUU

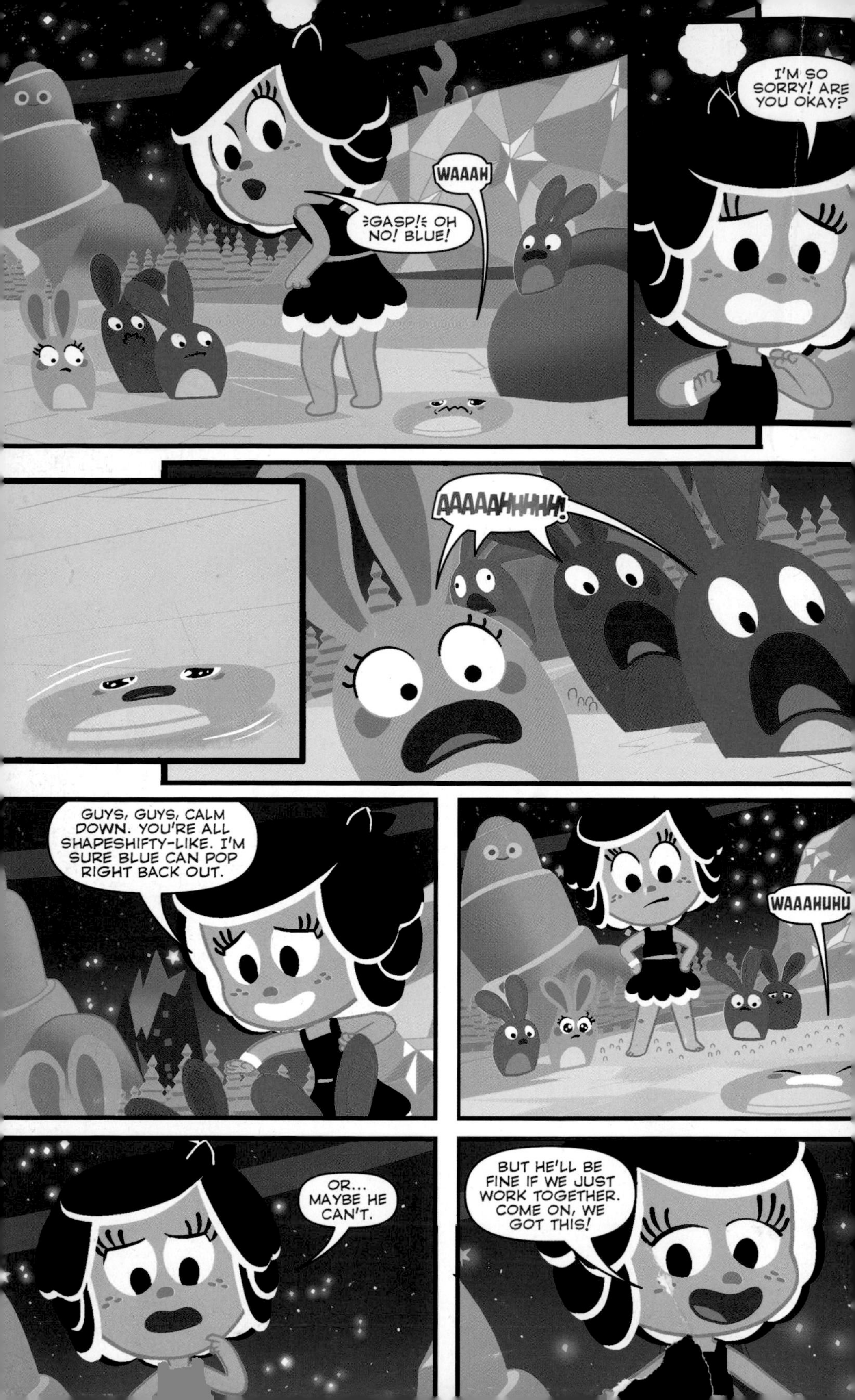

WAAAH
:GASP!: OH NO! BLUE!
I'M SO SORRY! ARE YOU OKAY?
AAAAAHHHHH!
GUYS, GUYS, CALM DOWN. YOU'RE ALL SHAPESHIFTY-LIKE. I'M SURE BLUE CAN POP RIGHT BACK OUT.
WAAAHUHU
OR... MAYBE HE CAN'T.
BUT HE'LL BE FINE IF WE JUST WORK TOGETHER. COME ON, WE GOT THIS!

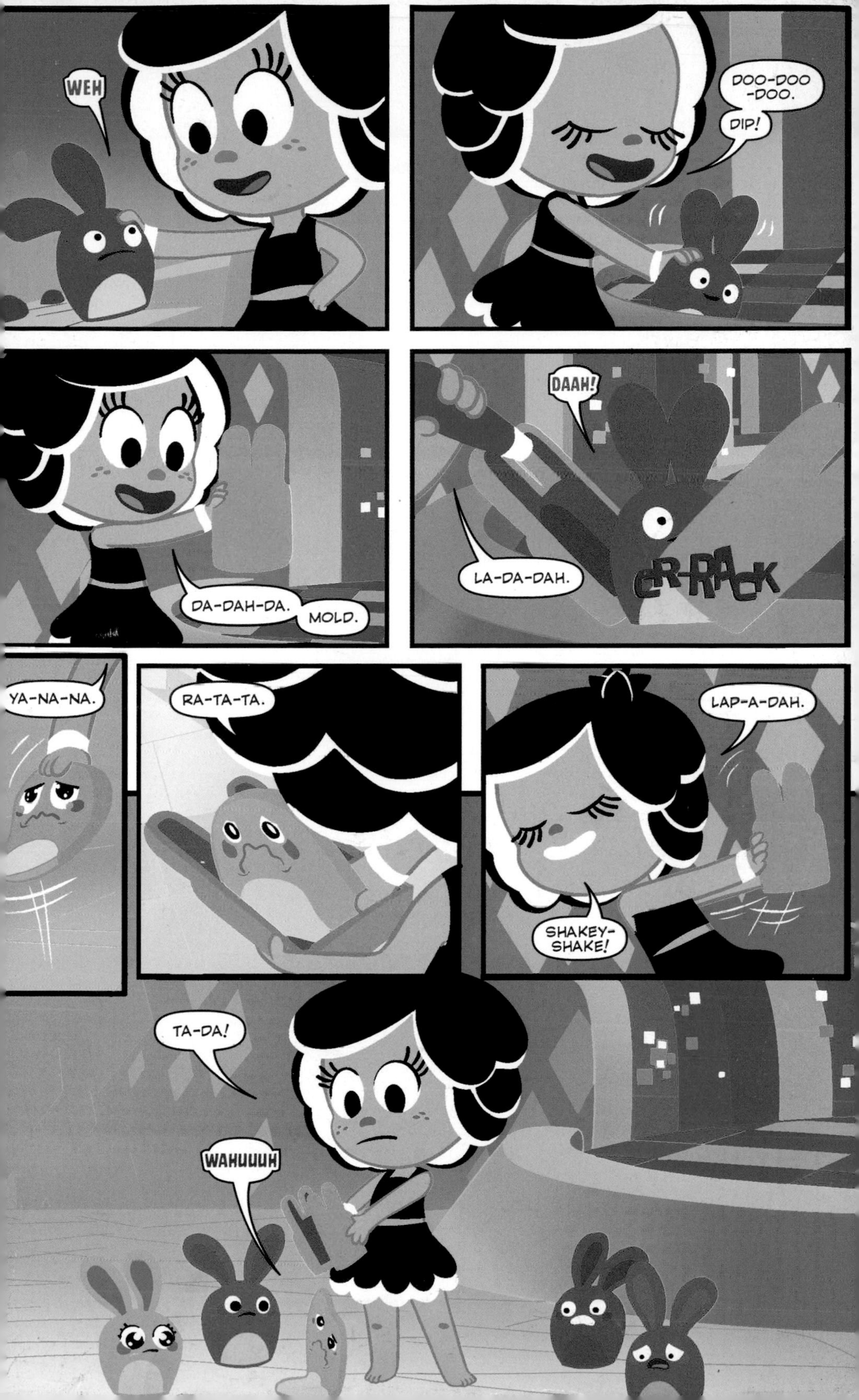
WEH
DOO-DOO -DOO.
DIP!
DA-DAH-DA.
MOLD.
DAAH!
LA-DA-DAH.
CR-RACK
YA-NA-NA.
RA-TA-TA.
LAP-A-DAH.
SHAKEY-SHAKE!
TA-DA!
WAHUUUH

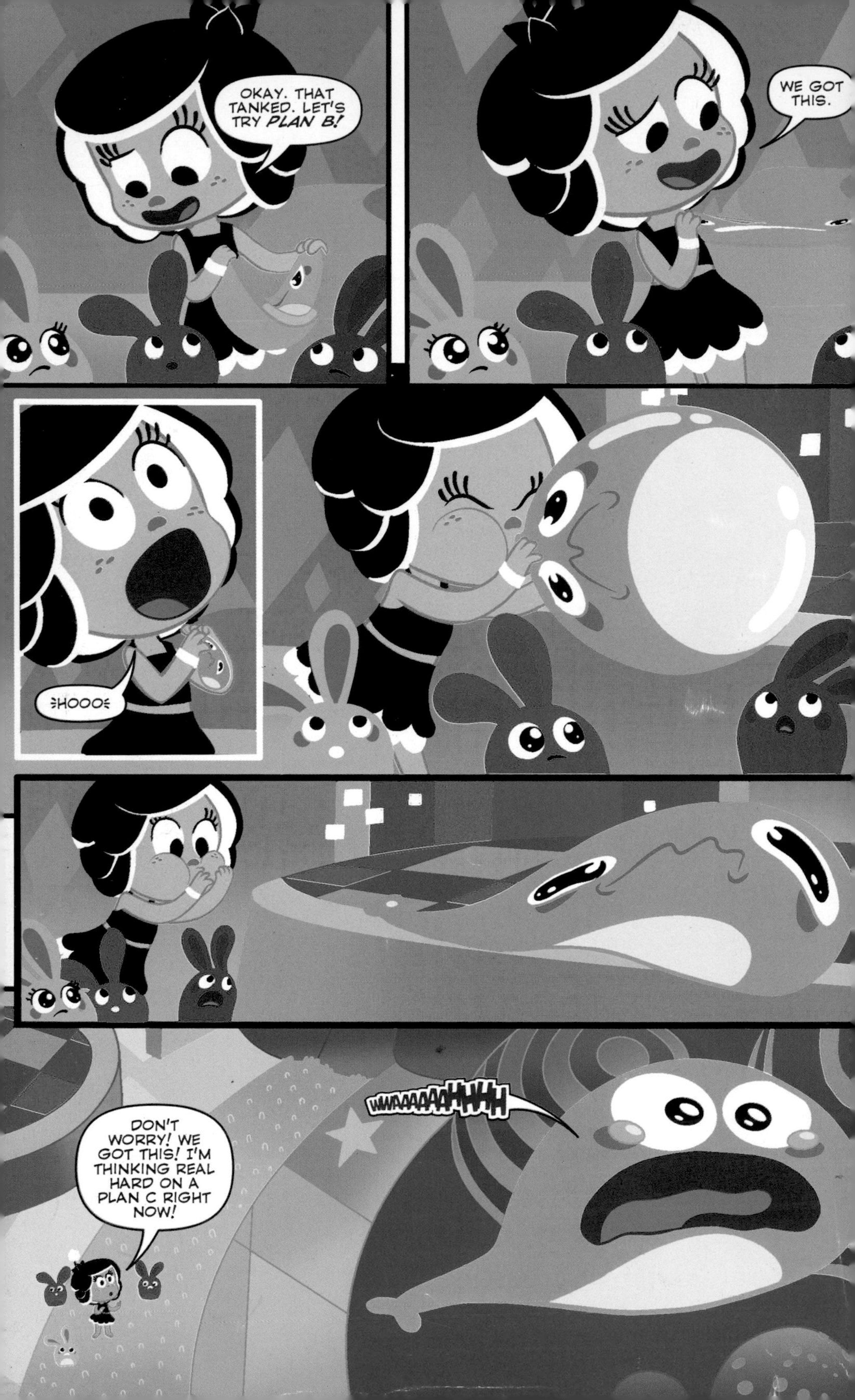
OKAY. THAT TANKED. LET'S TRY *PLAN B!*
WE GOT THIS.
HOOO
WWAAAAAAAHHHHH
DON'T WORRY! WE GOT THIS! I'M THINKING REAL HARD ON A PLAN C RIGHT NOW!

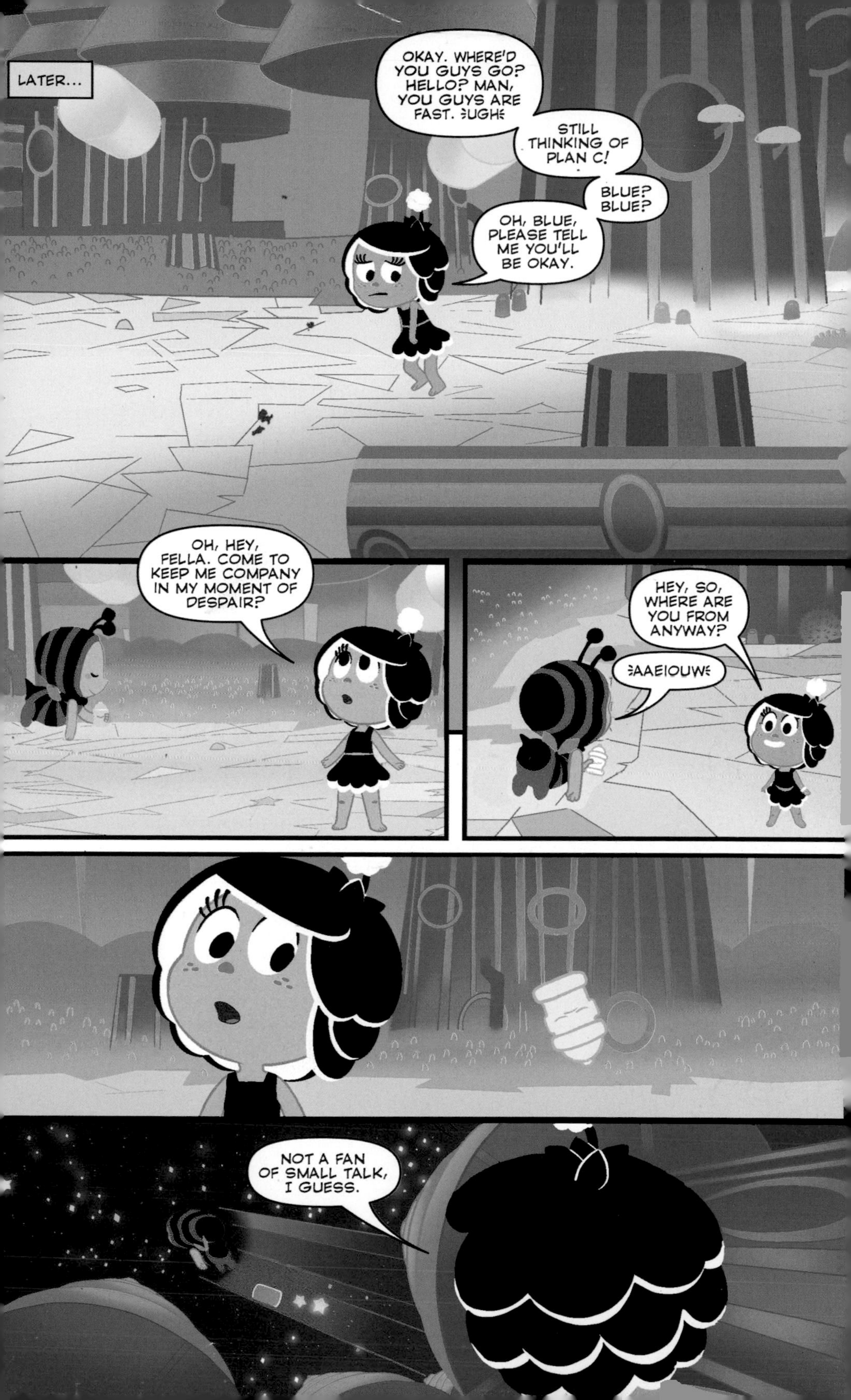
LATER...
OKAY. WHERE'D YOU GUYS GO? HELLO? MAN, YOU GUYS ARE FAST. UGH
STILL THINKING OF PLAN C!
BLUE? BLUE?
OH, BLUE, PLEASE TELL ME YOU'LL BE OKAY.
OH, HEY, FELLA. COME TO KEEP ME COMPANY IN MY MOMENT OF DESPAIR?
HEY, SO, WHERE ARE YOU FROM ANYWAY?
AAEIOUW
NOT A FAN OF SMALL TALK, I GUESS.

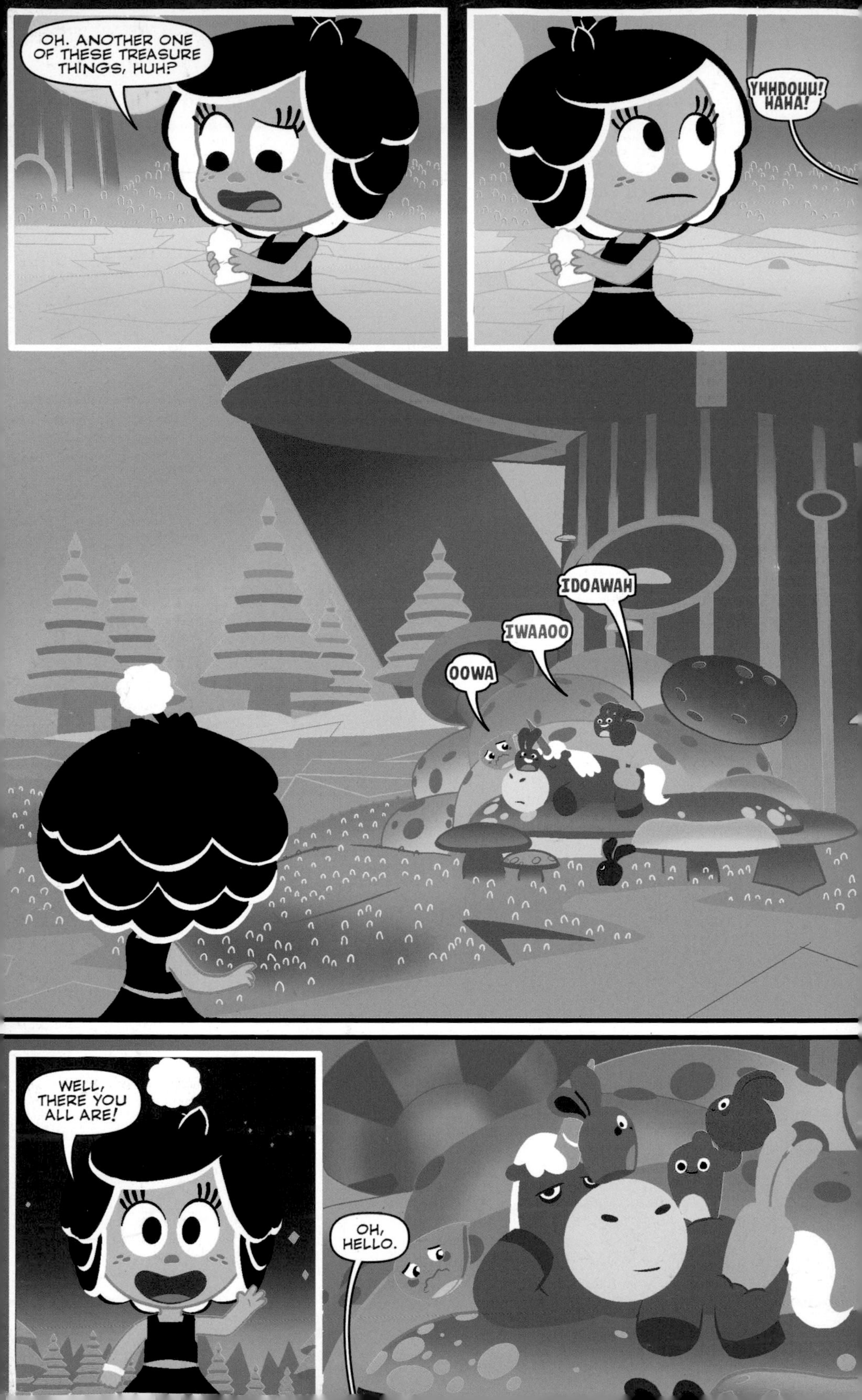
OH. ANOTHER ONE OF THESE TREASURE THINGS, HUH?
YHHDOUU! HAHA!
OOWA
IWAAOO
IDOAWAH
WELL, THERE YOU ALL ARE!
OH, HELLO.

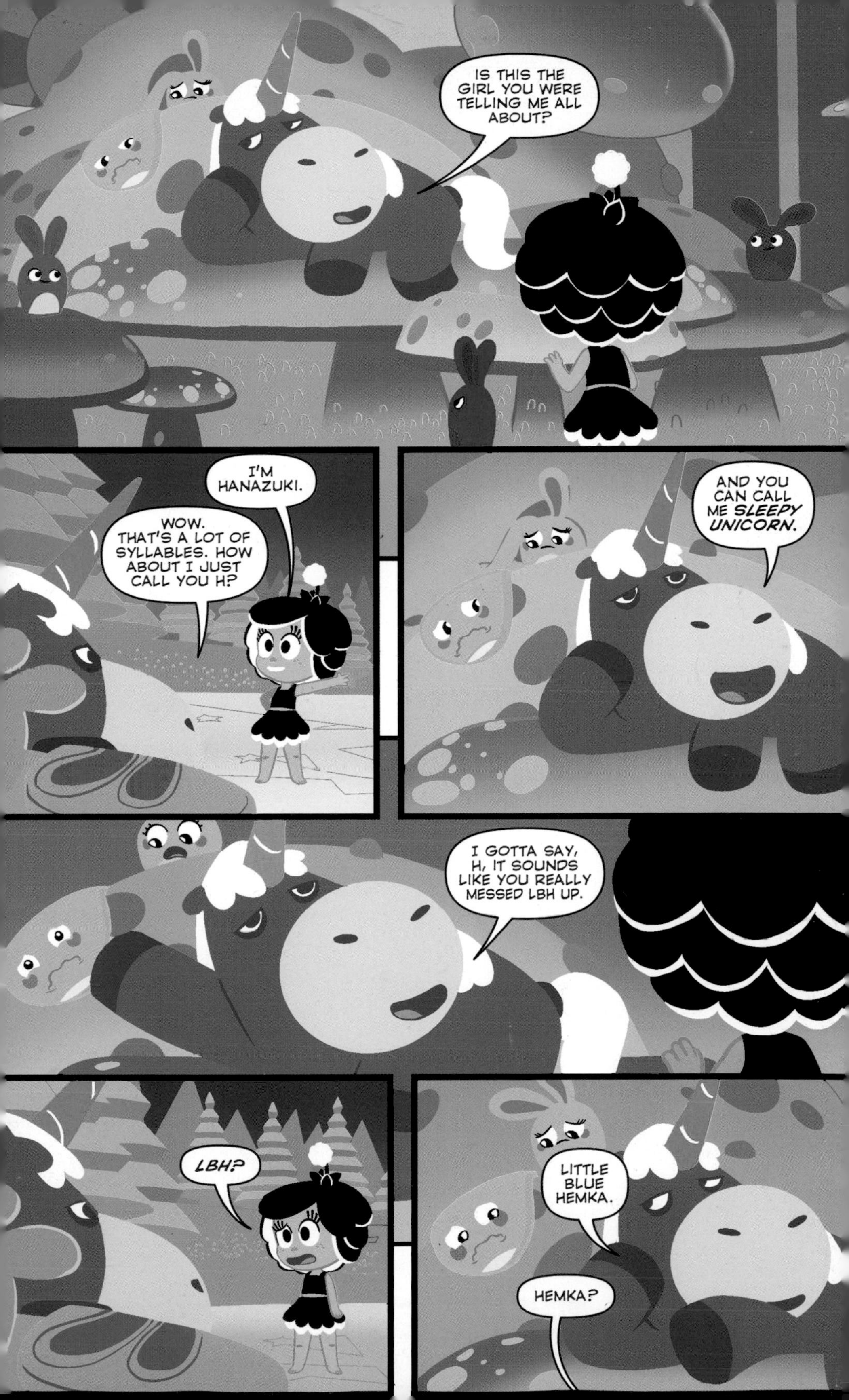
IS THIS THE GIRL YOU WERE TELLING ME ALL ABOUT?
I'M HANAZUKI.
WOW. THAT'S A LOT OF SYLLABLES. HOW ABOUT I JUST CALL YOU H?
AND YOU CAN CALL ME *SLEEPY UNICORN*.
I GOTTA SAY, H, IT SOUNDS LIKE YOU REALLY MESSED LBH UP.
LBH?
LITTLE BLUE HEMKA.
HEMKA?

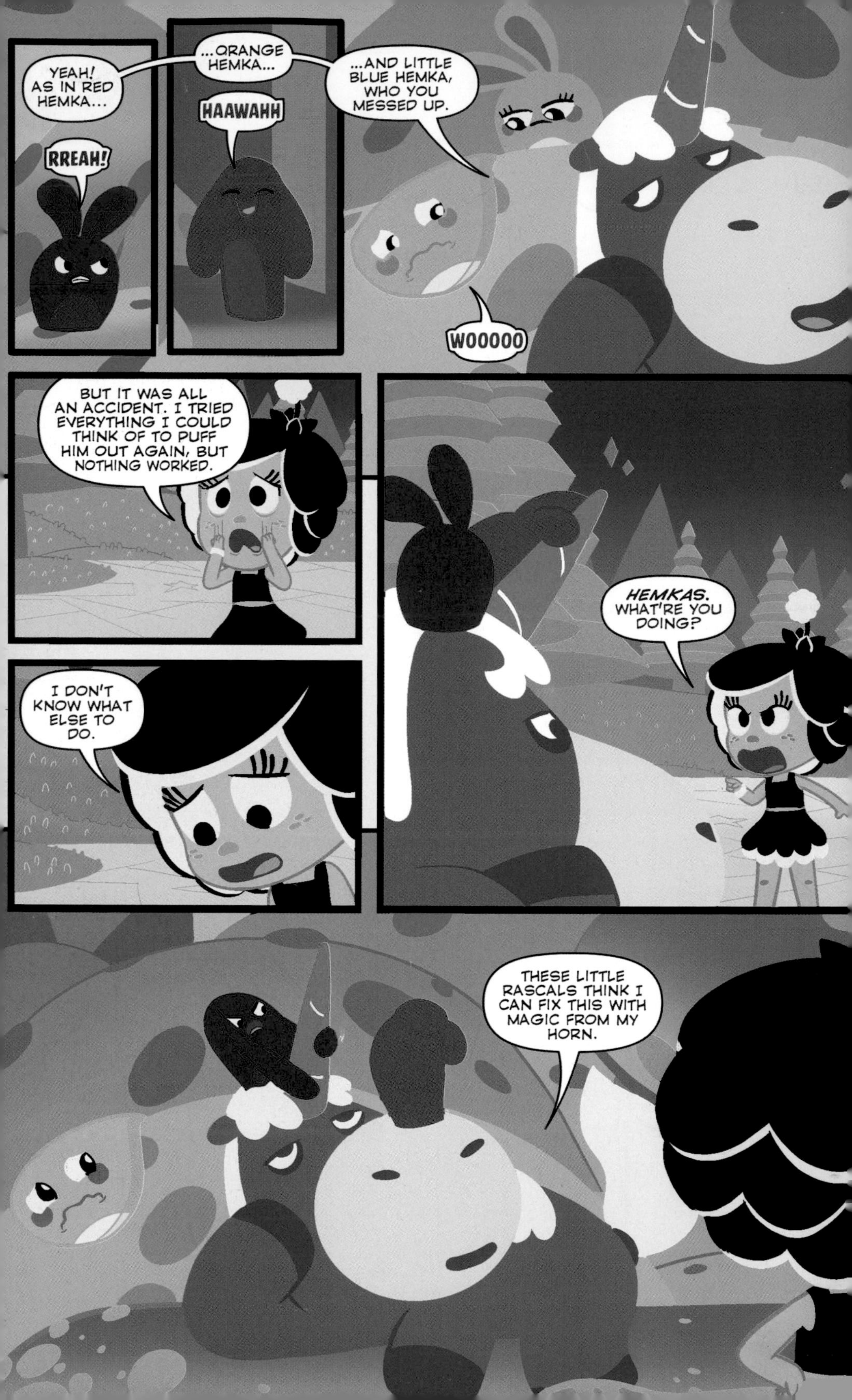
YEAH! AS IN RED HEMKA...
RREAH!
...ORANGE HEMKA...
HAAWAHH
...AND LITTLE BLUE HEMKA, WHO YOU MESSED UP.
WOOOOO
BUT IT WAS ALL AN ACCIDENT. I TRIED EVERYTHING I COULD THINK OF TO PUFF HIM OUT AGAIN, BUT NOTHING WORKED.
I DON'T KNOW WHAT ELSE TO DO.
HEMKAS. WHAT'RE YOU DOING?
THESE LITTLE RASCALS THINK I CAN FIX THIS WITH MAGIC FROM MY HORN.

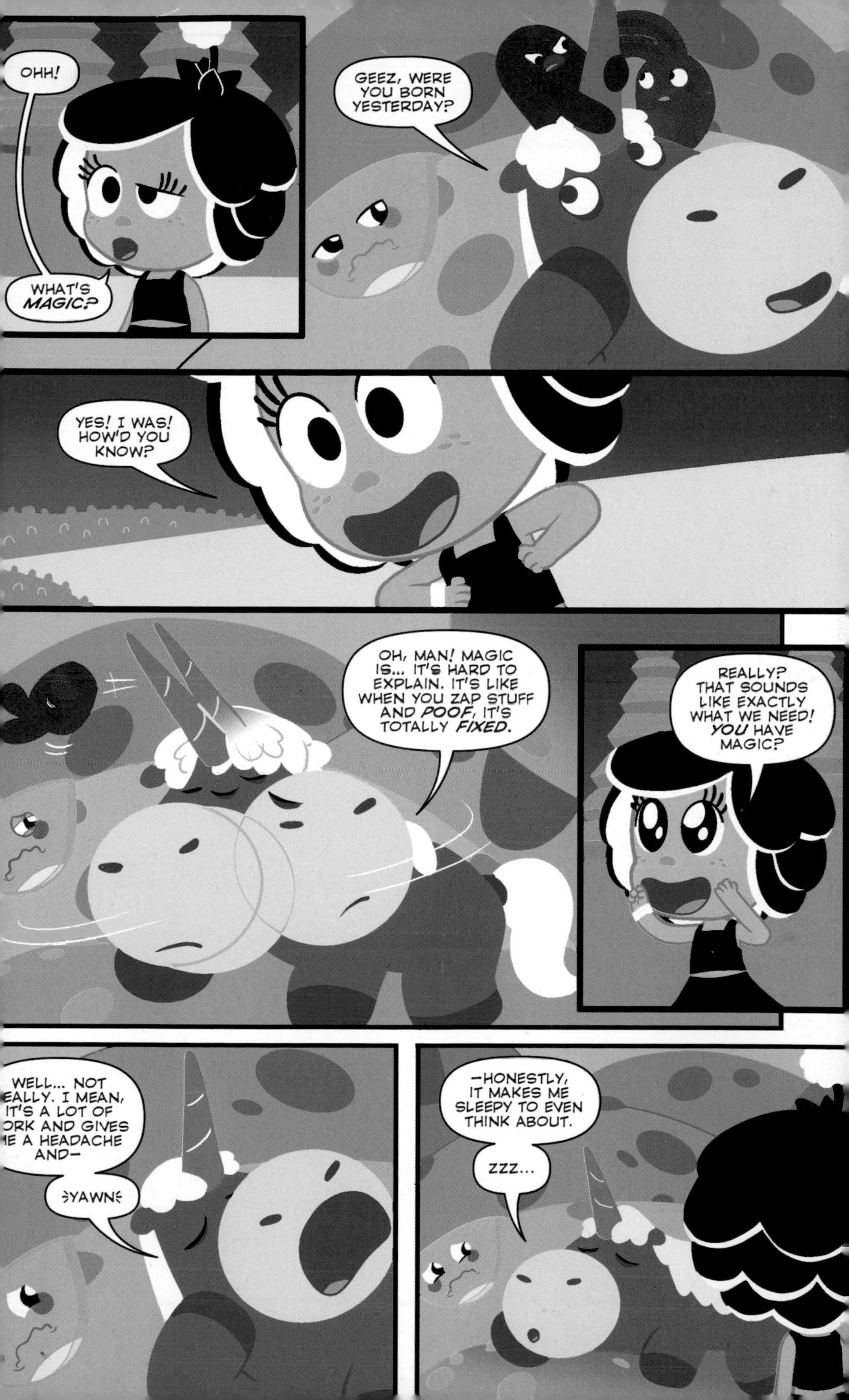
OHH!
WHAT'S *MAGIC?*
GEEZ, WERE YOU BORN YESTERDAY?
YES! I WAS! HOW'D YOU KNOW?
OH, MAN! MAGIC IS... IT'S HARD TO EXPLAIN. IT'S LIKE WHEN YOU ZAP STUFF AND *POOF*, IT'S TOTALLY *FIXED*.
REALLY? THAT SOUNDS LIKE EXACTLY WHAT WE NEED! *YOU* HAVE MAGIC?
WELL... NOT EALLY. I MEAN, IT'S A LOT OF ORK AND GIVES E A HEADACHE AND—
YAWN
—HONESTLY, IT MAKES ME SLEEPY TO EVEN THINK ABOUT.
ZZZ...

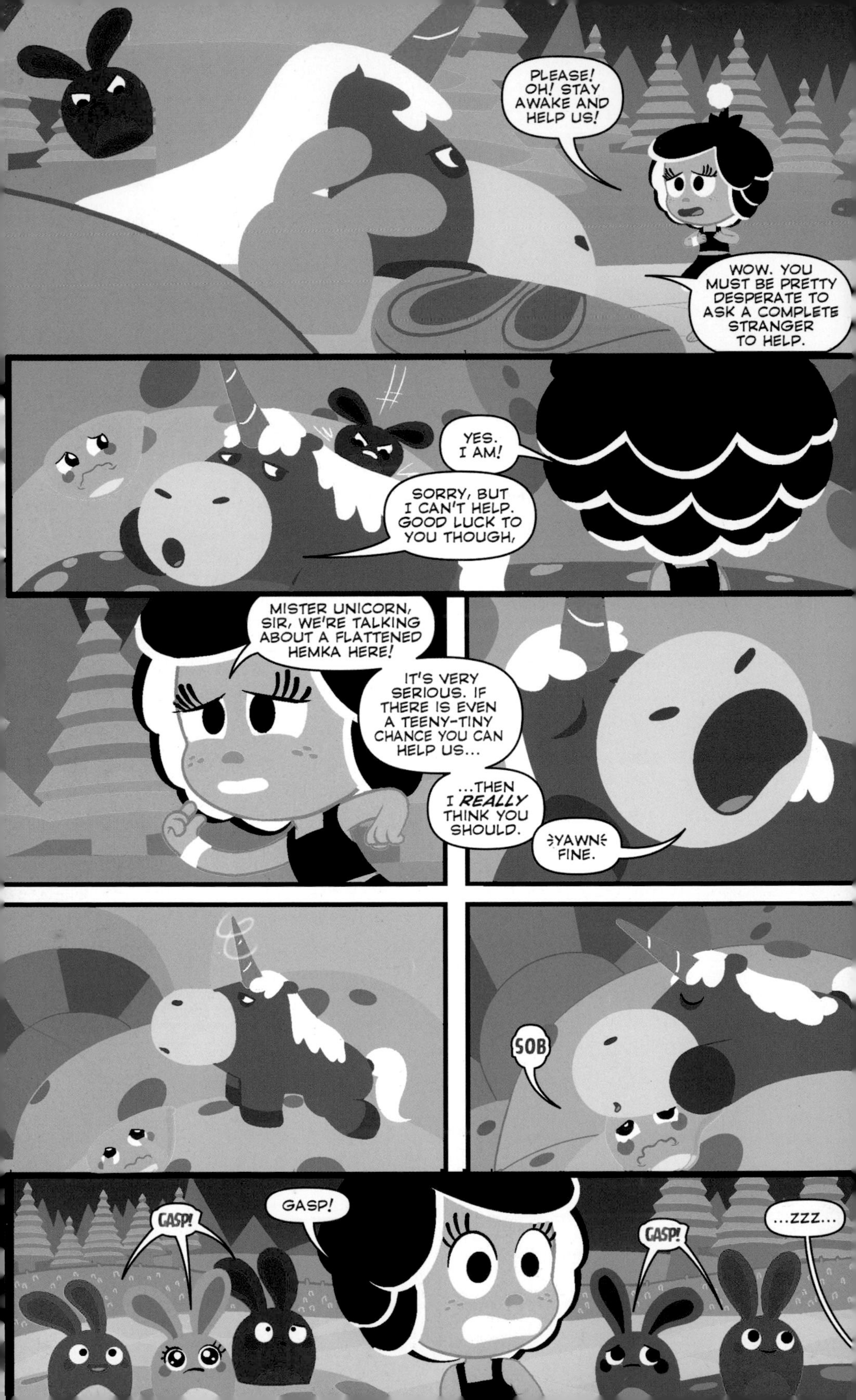
PLEASE! OH! STAY AWAKE AND HELP US!
WOW. YOU MUST BE PRETTY DESPERATE TO ASK A COMPLETE STRANGER TO HELP.
YES. I AM!
SORRY, BUT I CAN'T HELP. GOOD LUCK TO YOU THOUGH.
MISTER UNICORN, SIR, WE'RE TALKING ABOUT A FLATTENED HEMKA HERE!
IT'S VERY SERIOUS. IF THERE IS EVEN A TEENY-TINY CHANCE YOU CAN HELP US...
...THEN I REALLY THINK YOU SHOULD.
YAWN FINE.
SOB
GASP!
GASP!
GASP!
...ZZZ...

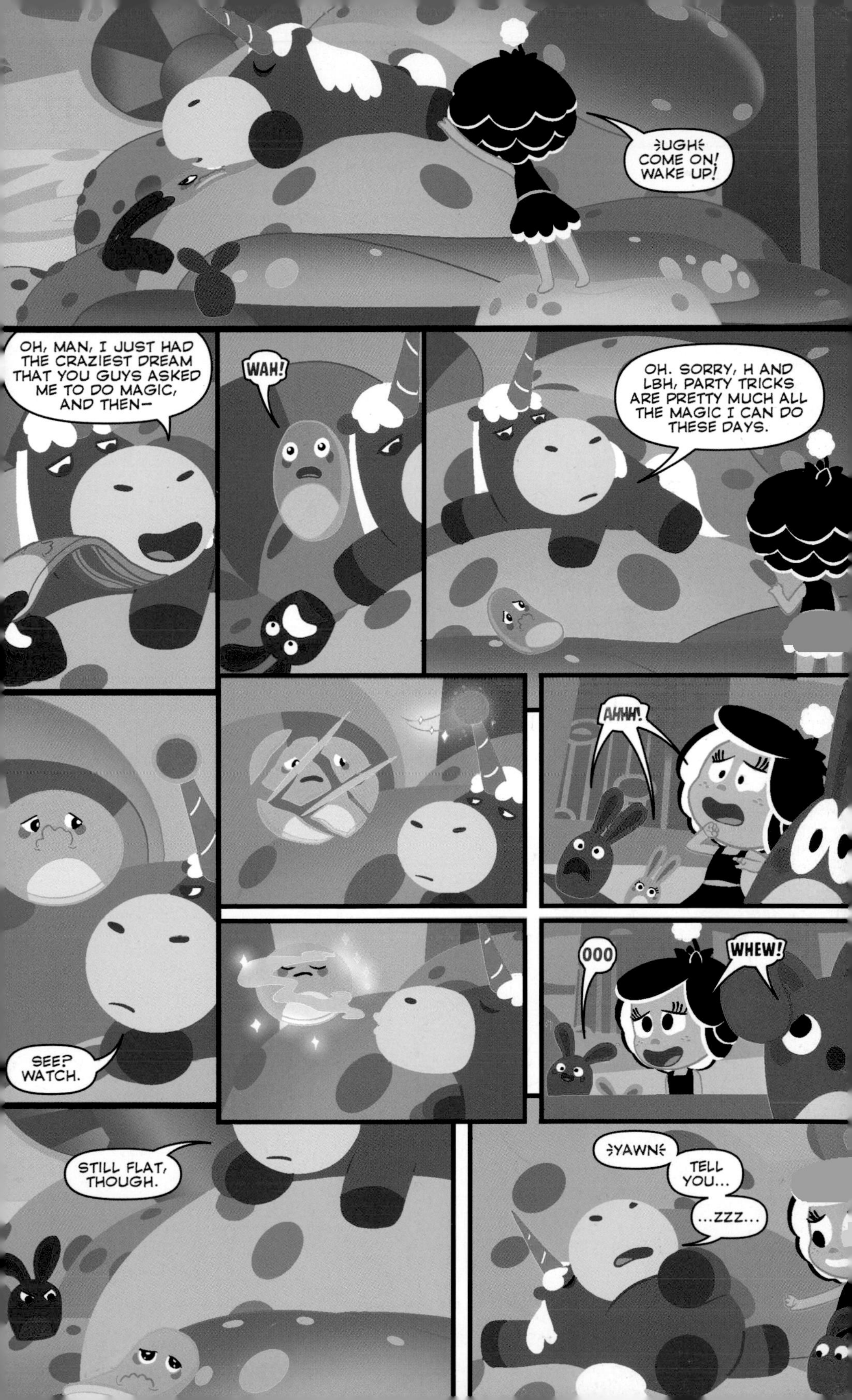

⩤UGH⩥ COME ON! WAKE UP!
OH, MAN, I JUST HAD THE CRAZIEST DREAM THAT YOU GUYS ASKED ME TO DO MAGIC, AND THEN—
WAH!
OH. SORRY, H AND LBH, PARTY TRICKS ARE PRETTY MUCH ALL THE MAGIC I CAN DO THESE DAYS.
SEE? WATCH.
AHHH!
OOO
WHEW!
STILL FLAT, THOUGH.
⩤YAWN⩥
TELL YOU...
...ZZZ...

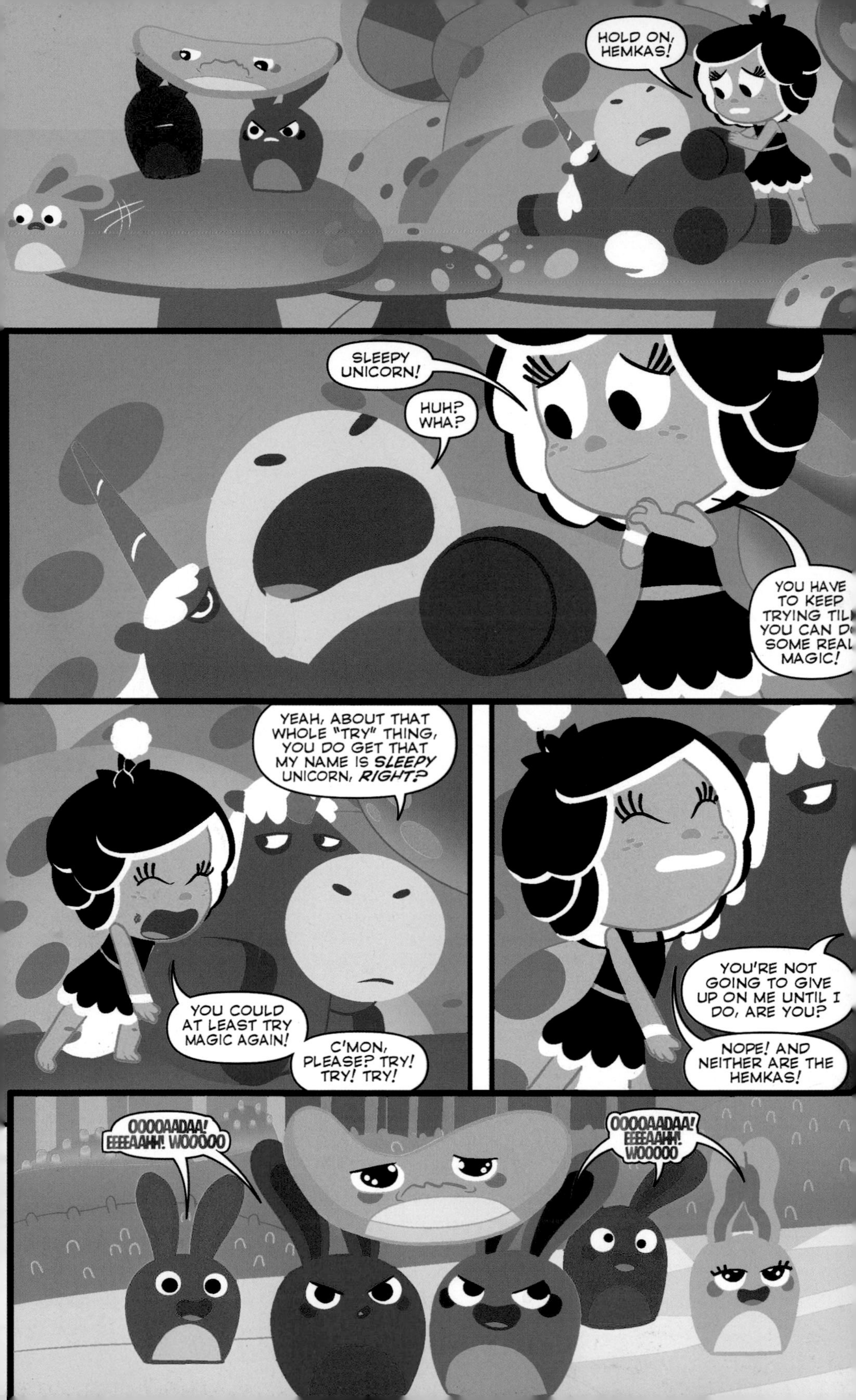
HOLD ON, HEMKAS!
SLEEPY UNICORN!
HUH? WHA?
YOU HAVE TO KEEP TRYING TILL YOU CAN DO SOME REAL MAGIC!
YEAH, ABOUT THAT WHOLE "TRY" THING, YOU DO GET THAT MY NAME IS SLEEPY UNICORN, RIGHT?
YOU COULD AT LEAST TRY MAGIC AGAIN!
C'MON, PLEASE? TRY! TRY! TRY!
YOU'RE NOT GOING TO GIVE UP ON ME UNTIL I DO, ARE YOU?
NOPE! AND NEITHER ARE THE HEMKAS!
OOOOAADAA! EEEEAAHH! WOOOOO
OOOOAADAA! EEEEAAHH! WOOOOO

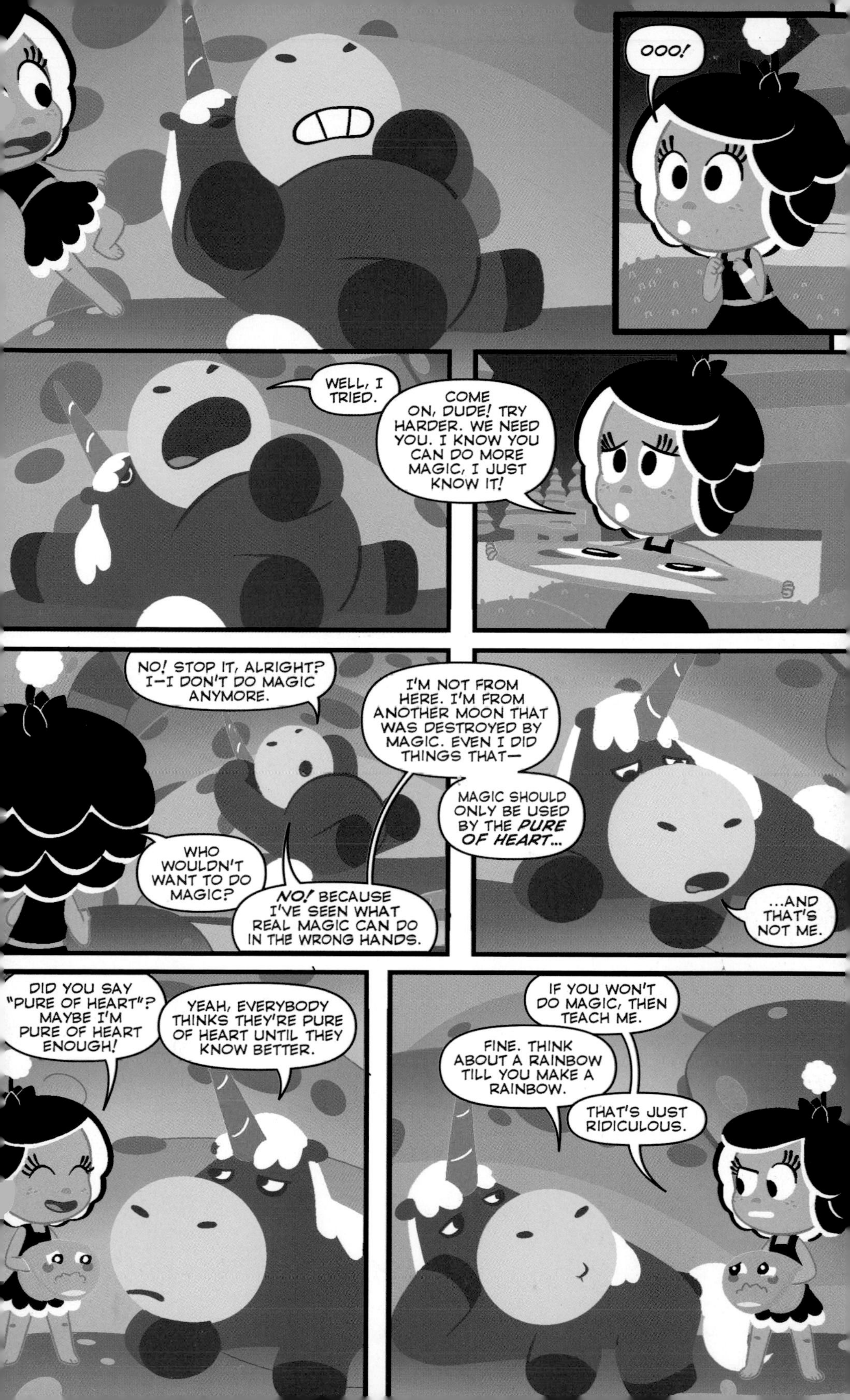
OOO!
WELL, I TRIED.
COME ON, DUDE! TRY HARDER. WE NEED YOU. I KNOW YOU CAN DO MORE MAGIC, I JUST KNOW IT!
NO! STOP IT, ALRIGHT? I—I DON'T DO MAGIC ANYMORE.
WHO WOULDN'T WANT TO DO MAGIC?
NO! BECAUSE I'VE SEEN WHAT REAL MAGIC CAN DO IN THE WRONG HANDS.
I'M NOT FROM HERE. I'M FROM ANOTHER MOON THAT WAS DESTROYED BY MAGIC. EVEN I DID THINGS THAT—
MAGIC SHOULD ONLY BE USED BY THE PURE OF HEART...
...AND THAT'S NOT ME.
DID YOU SAY "PURE OF HEART"? MAYBE I'M PURE OF HEART ENOUGH!
YEAH, EVERYBODY THINKS THEY'RE PURE OF HEART UNTIL THEY KNOW BETTER.
IF YOU WON'T DO MAGIC, THEN TEACH ME.
FINE. THINK ABOUT A RAINBOW TILL YOU MAKE A RAINBOW.
THAT'S JUST RIDICULOUS.

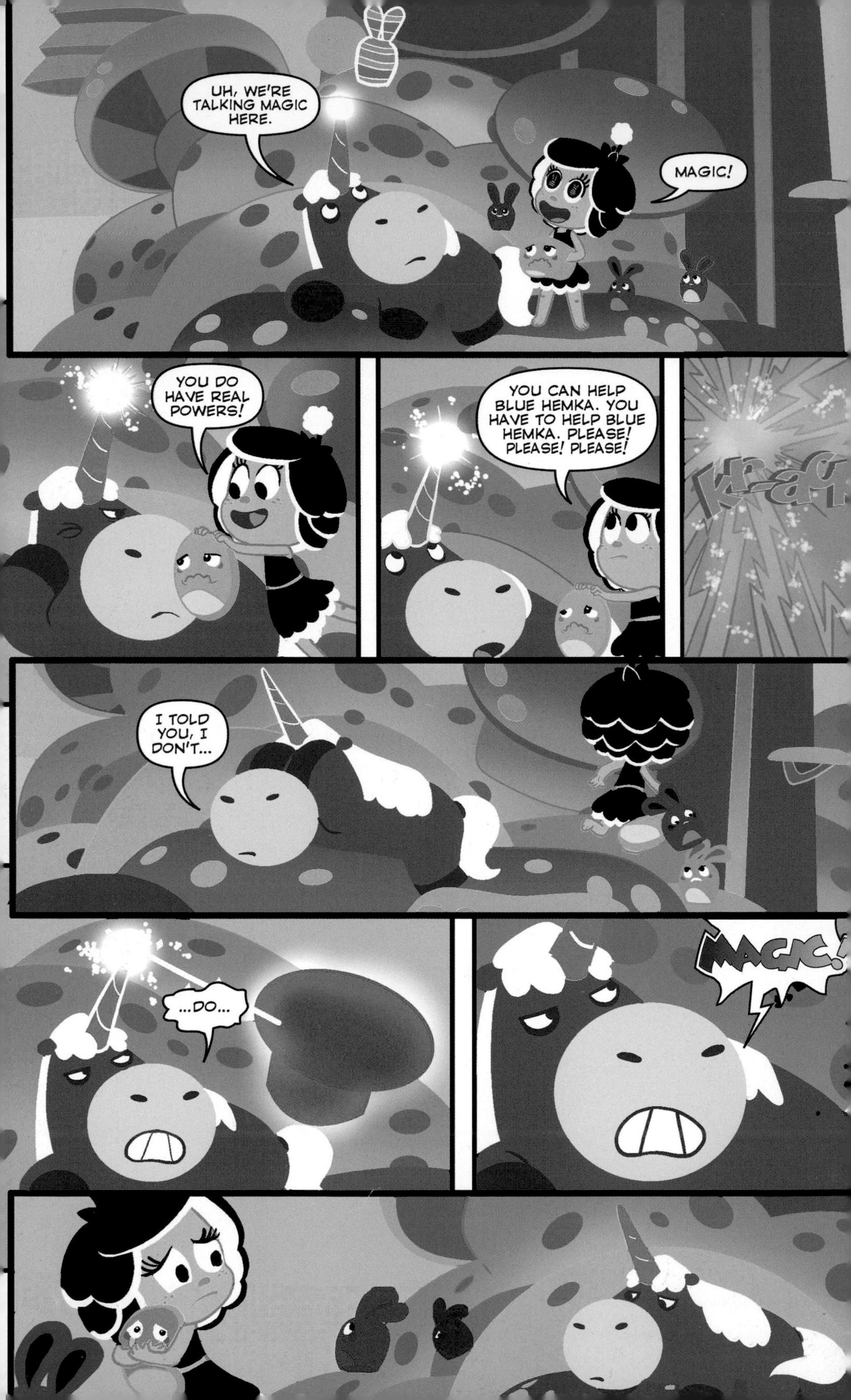
UH, WE'RE TALKING MAGIC HERE.
MAGIC!
YOU DO HAVE REAL POWERS!
YOU CAN HELP BLUE HEMKA. YOU HAVE TO HELP BLUE HEMKA. PLEASE! PLEASE! PLEASE!
I TOLD YOU, I DON'T...
...DO...
MAGIC!

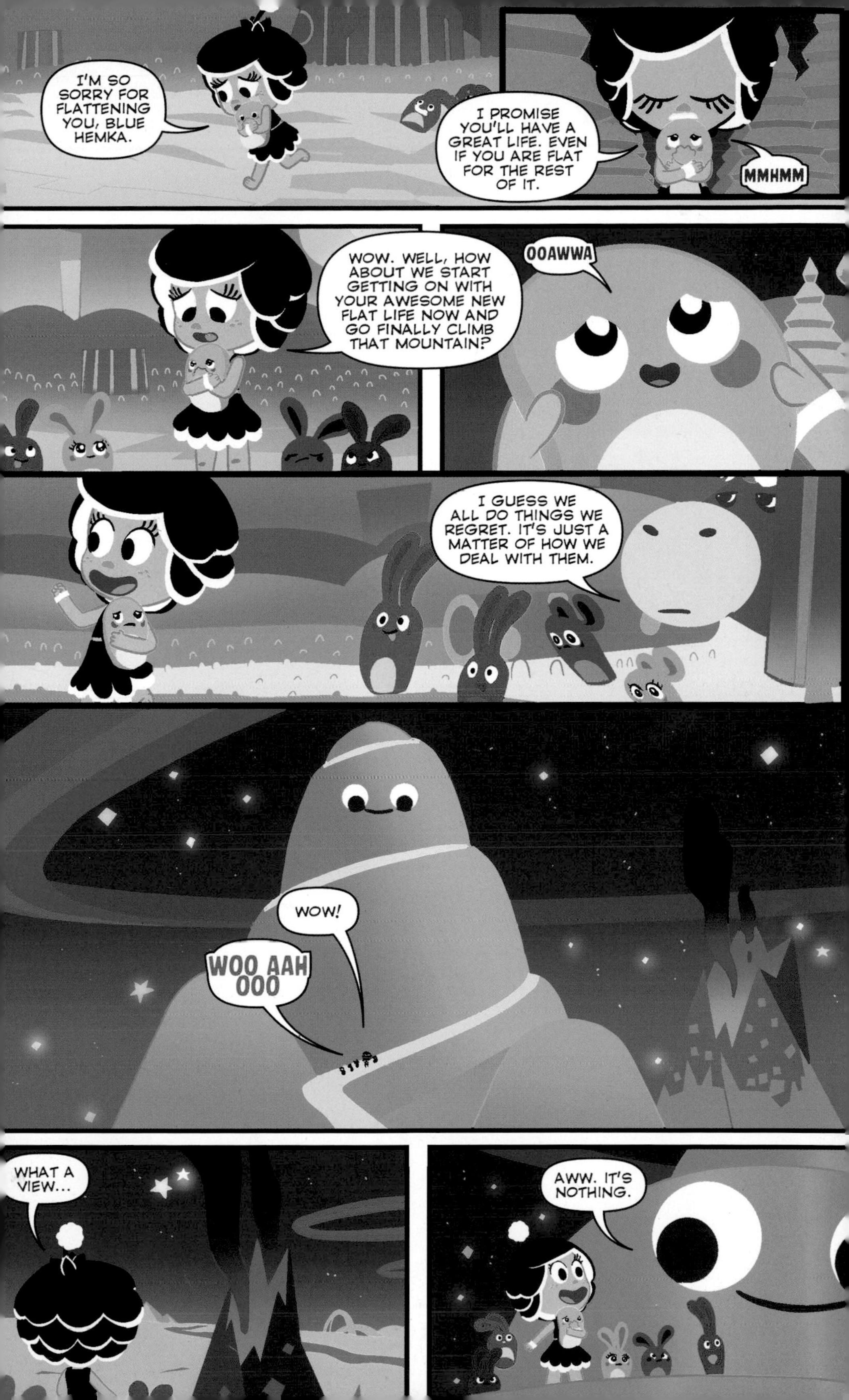
I'M SO SORRY FOR FLATTENING YOU, BLUE HEMKA.
I PROMISE YOU'LL HAVE A GREAT LIFE. EVEN IF YOU ARE FLAT FOR THE REST OF IT.
MMHMM
WOW. WELL, HOW ABOUT WE START GETTING ON WITH YOUR AWESOME NEW FLAT LIFE NOW AND GO FINALLY CLIMB THAT MOUNTAIN?
OOAWWA
I GUESS WE ALL DO THINGS WE REGRET. IT'S JUST A MATTER OF HOW WE DEAL WITH THEM.
WOW!
WOO AAH OOO
WHAT A VIEW...
AWW. IT'S NOTHING.

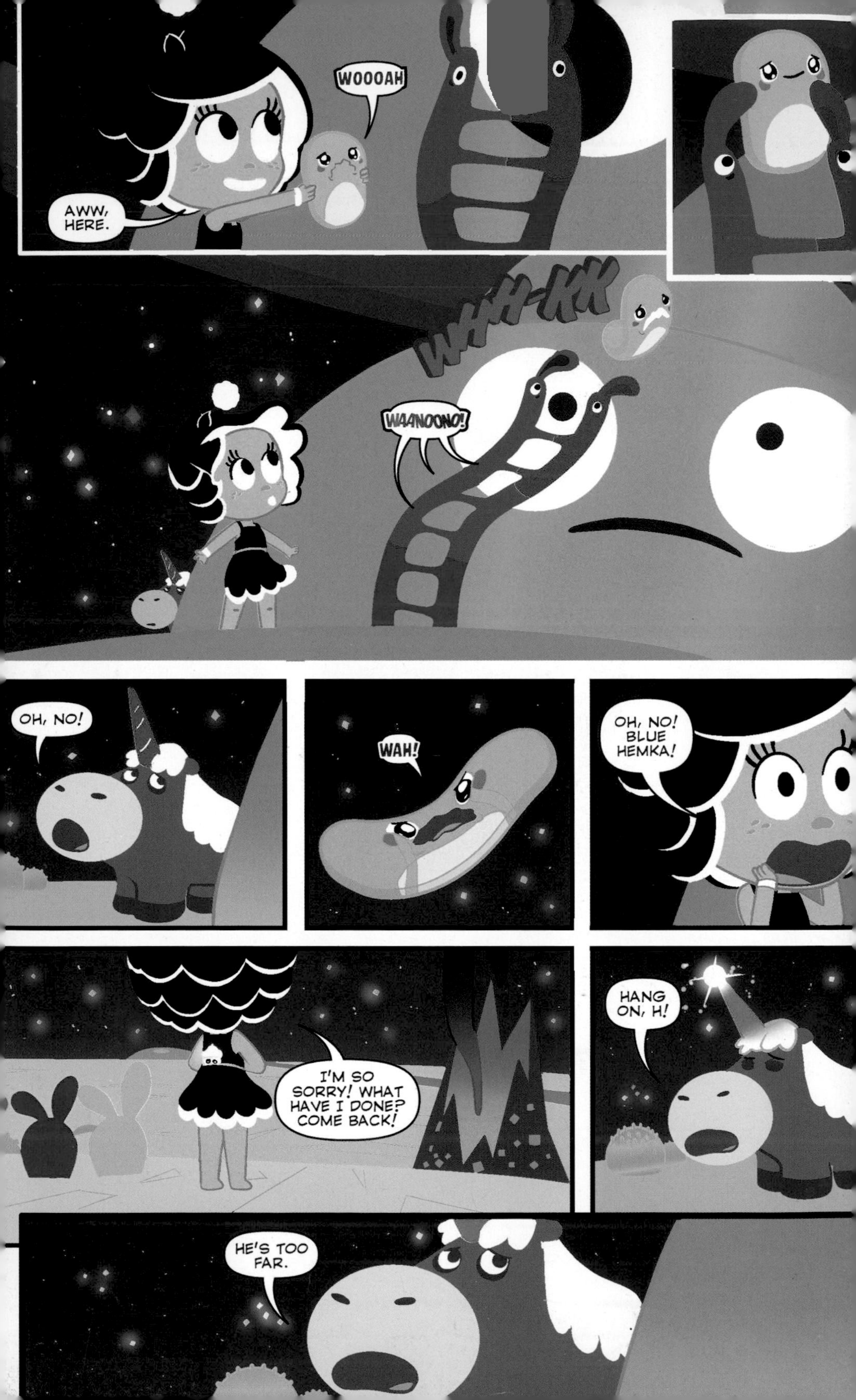
WOOOAH
AWW, HERE.
WHH-KK
WAANOONO!
OH, NO!
WAH!
OH, NO! BLUE HEMKA!
I'M SO SORRY! WHAT HAVE I DONE? COME BACK!
HANG ON, H!
HE'S TOO FAR.

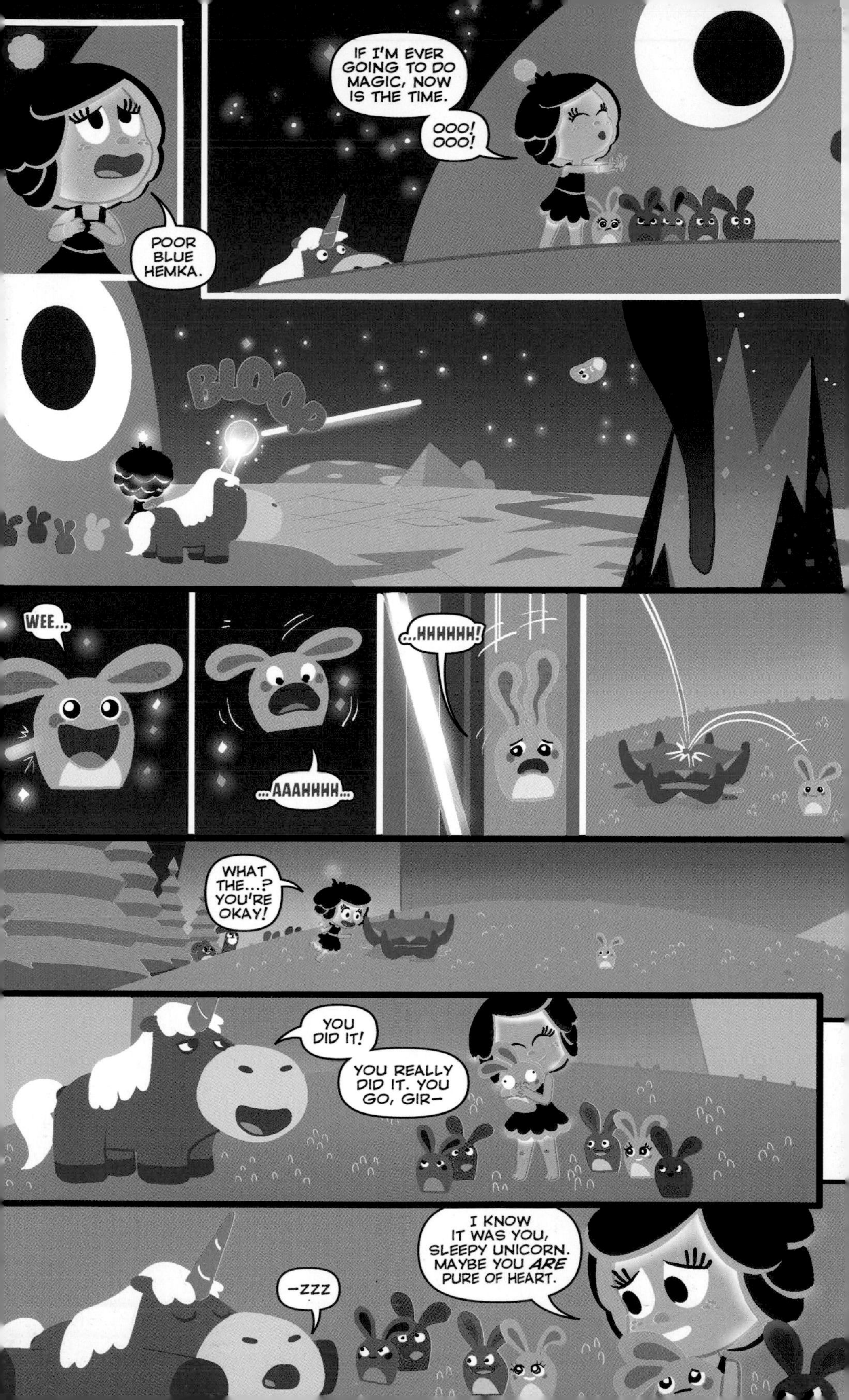
POOR BLUE HEMKA.
IF I'M EVER GOING TO DO MAGIC, NOW IS THE TIME.
OOO! OOO!
BLOOP
WEE...
...AAAHHHH...
...HHHHHH!
WHAT THE...? YOU'RE OKAY!
YOU DID IT!
YOU REALLY DID IT. YOU GO, GIR–
–ZZZ
I KNOW IT WAS YOU, SLEEPY UNICORN. MAYBE YOU *ARE* PURE OF HEART.

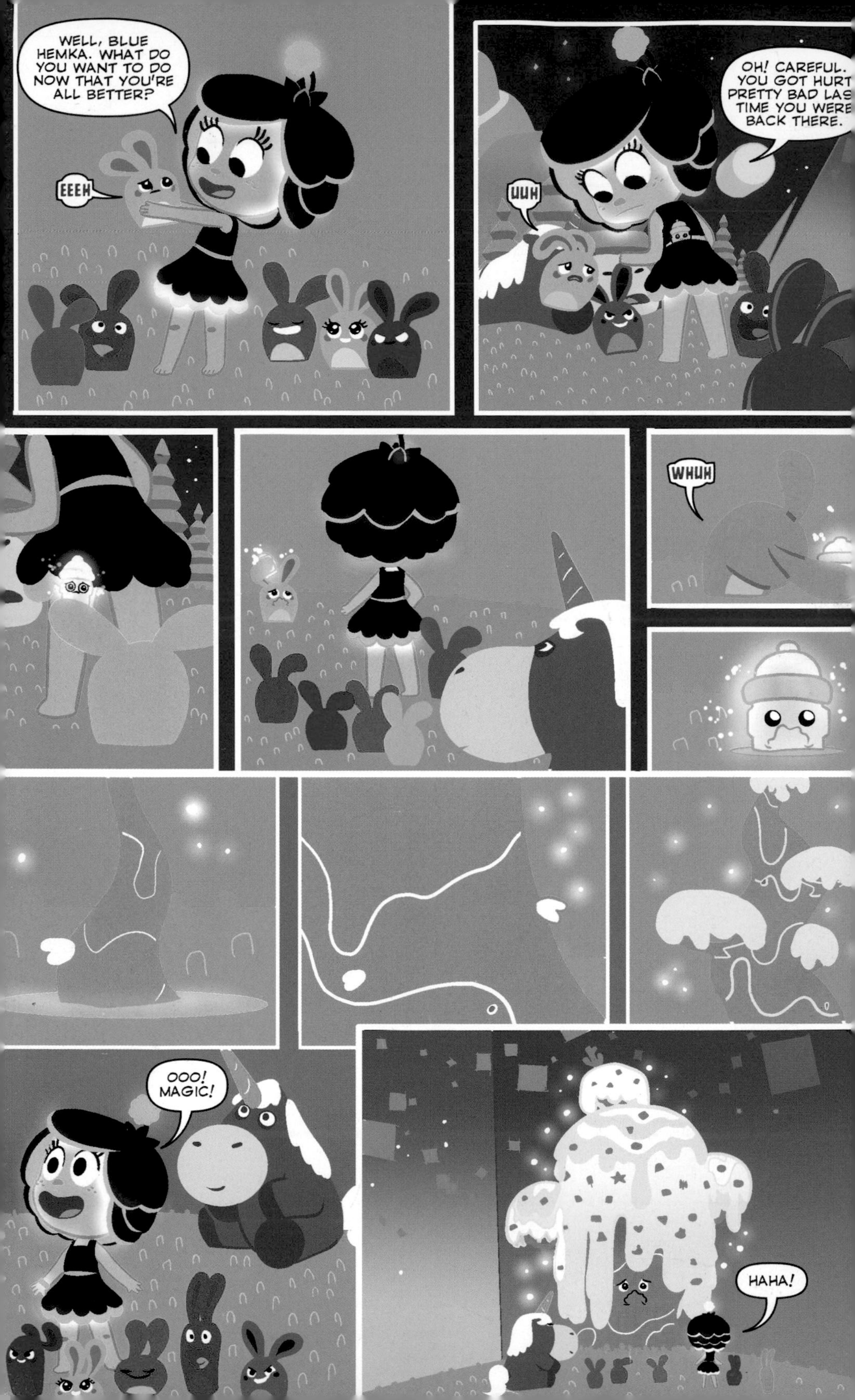
WELL, BLUE HEMKA. WHAT DO YOU WANT TO DO NOW THAT YOU'RE ALL BETTER?
EEEH
OH! CAREFUL. YOU GOT HURT PRETTY BAD LAS TIME YOU WERE BACK THERE.
UUH
WHUH
OOO! MAGIC!
HAHA!

COVER ART BY **YASMIN SHIEKH**

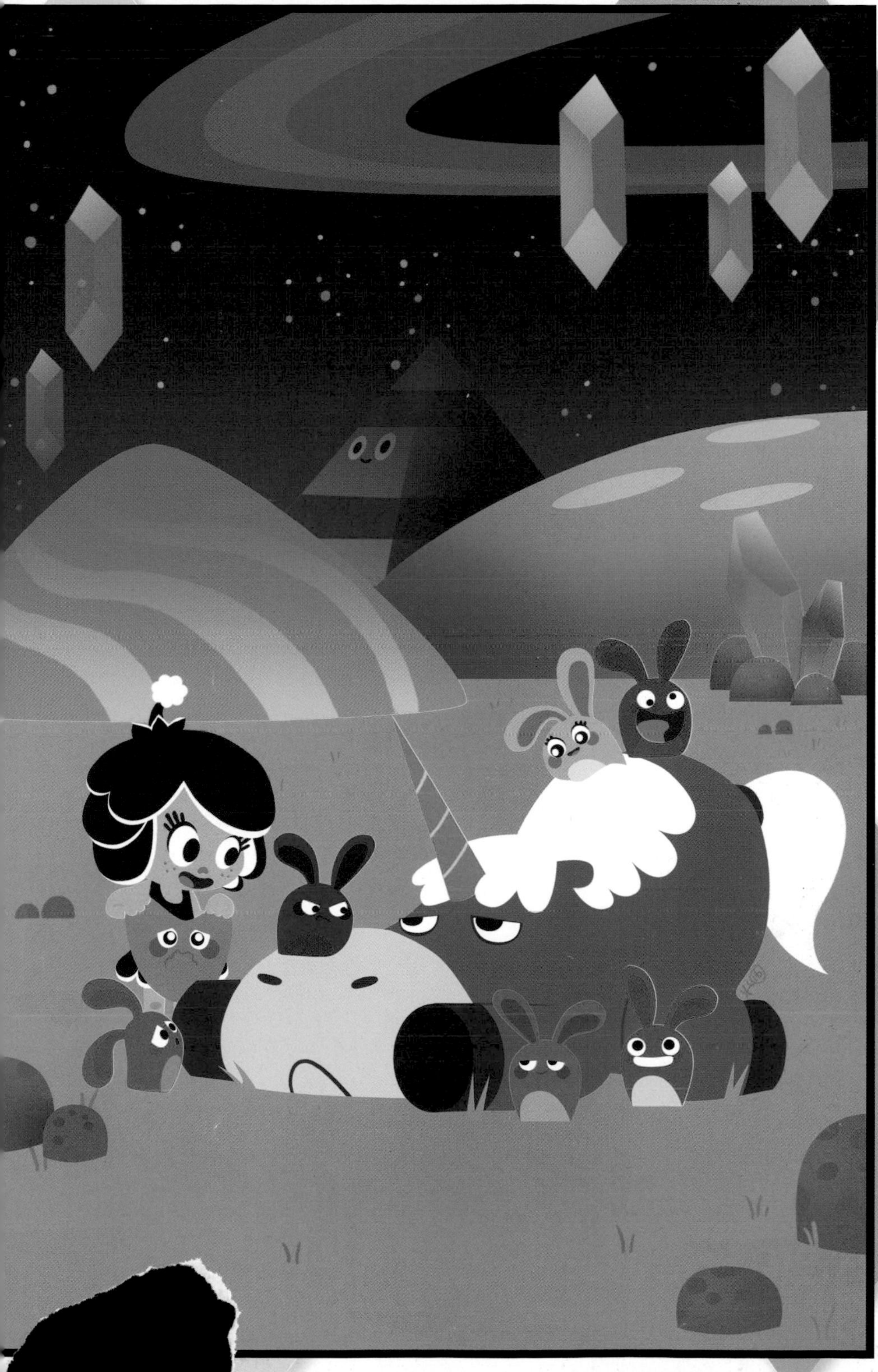

COVER ART BY **NICO PEÑA** COLORS BY **VALENTINA PINTO**

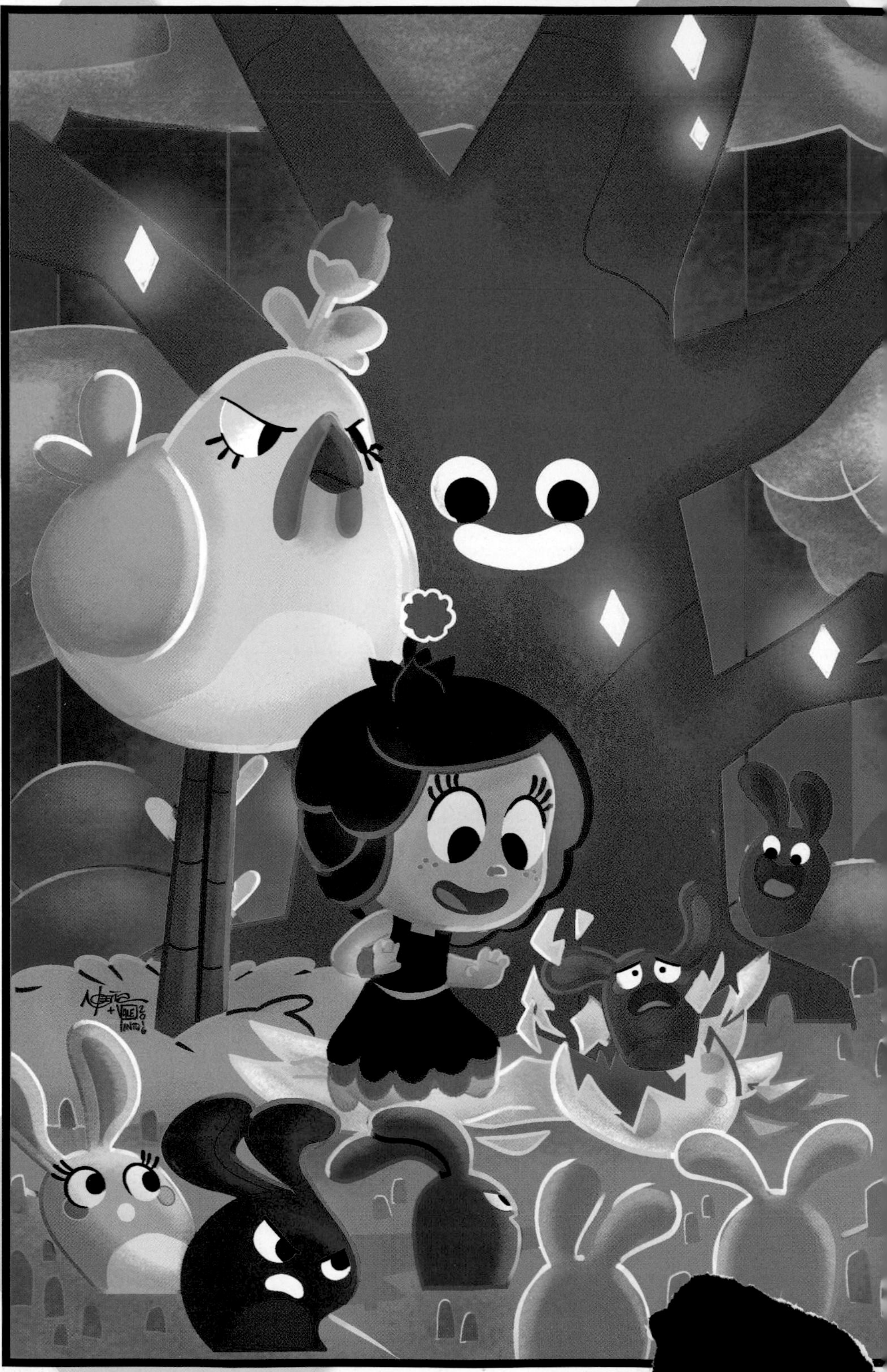

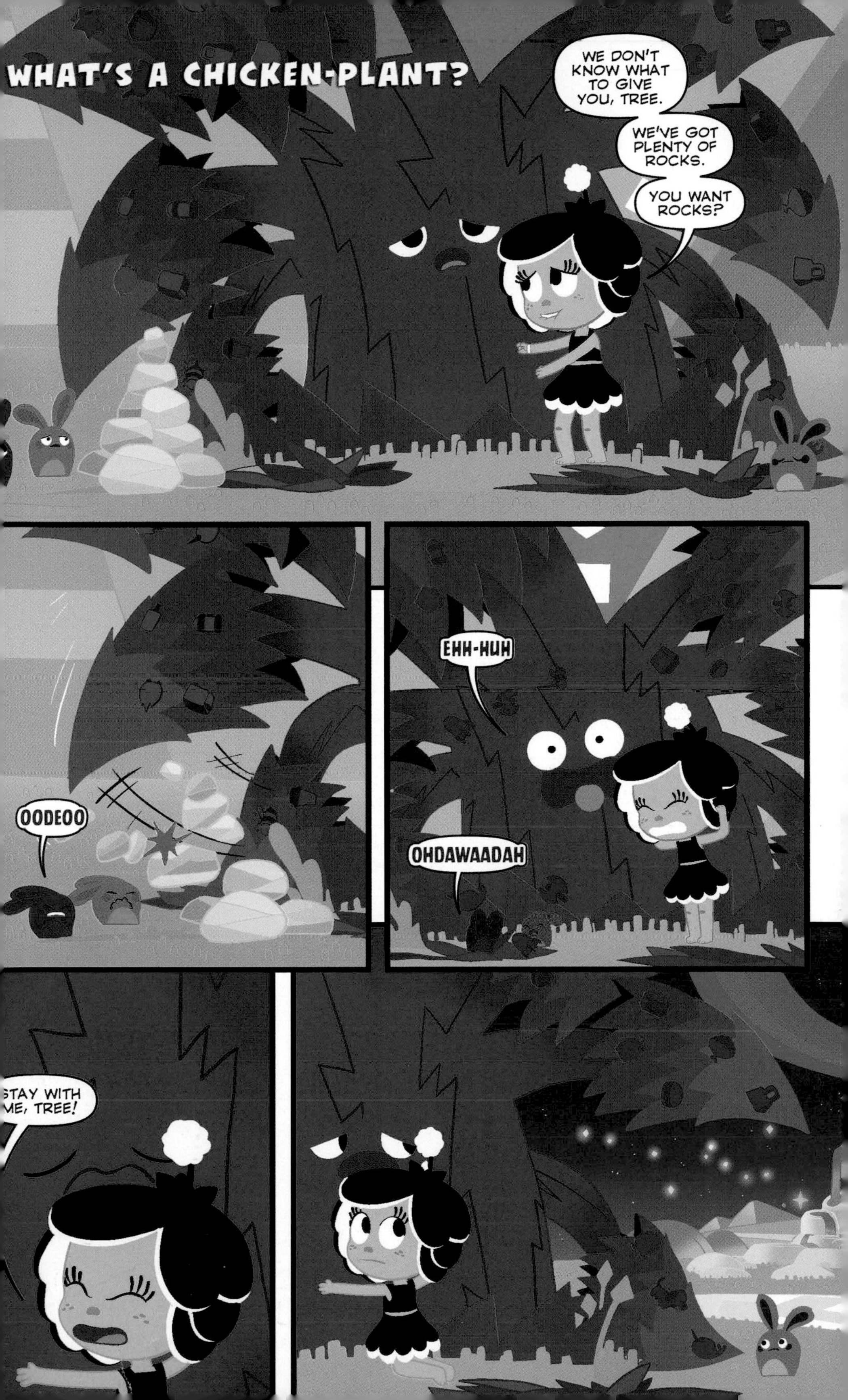
WHAT'S A CHICKEN-PLANT?
WE DON'T KNOW WHAT TO GIVE YOU, TREE.
WE'VE GOT PLENTY OF ROCKS.
YOU WANT ROCKS?
OODEOO
EHH-HUH
OHDAWAADAH
STAY WITH ME, TREE!

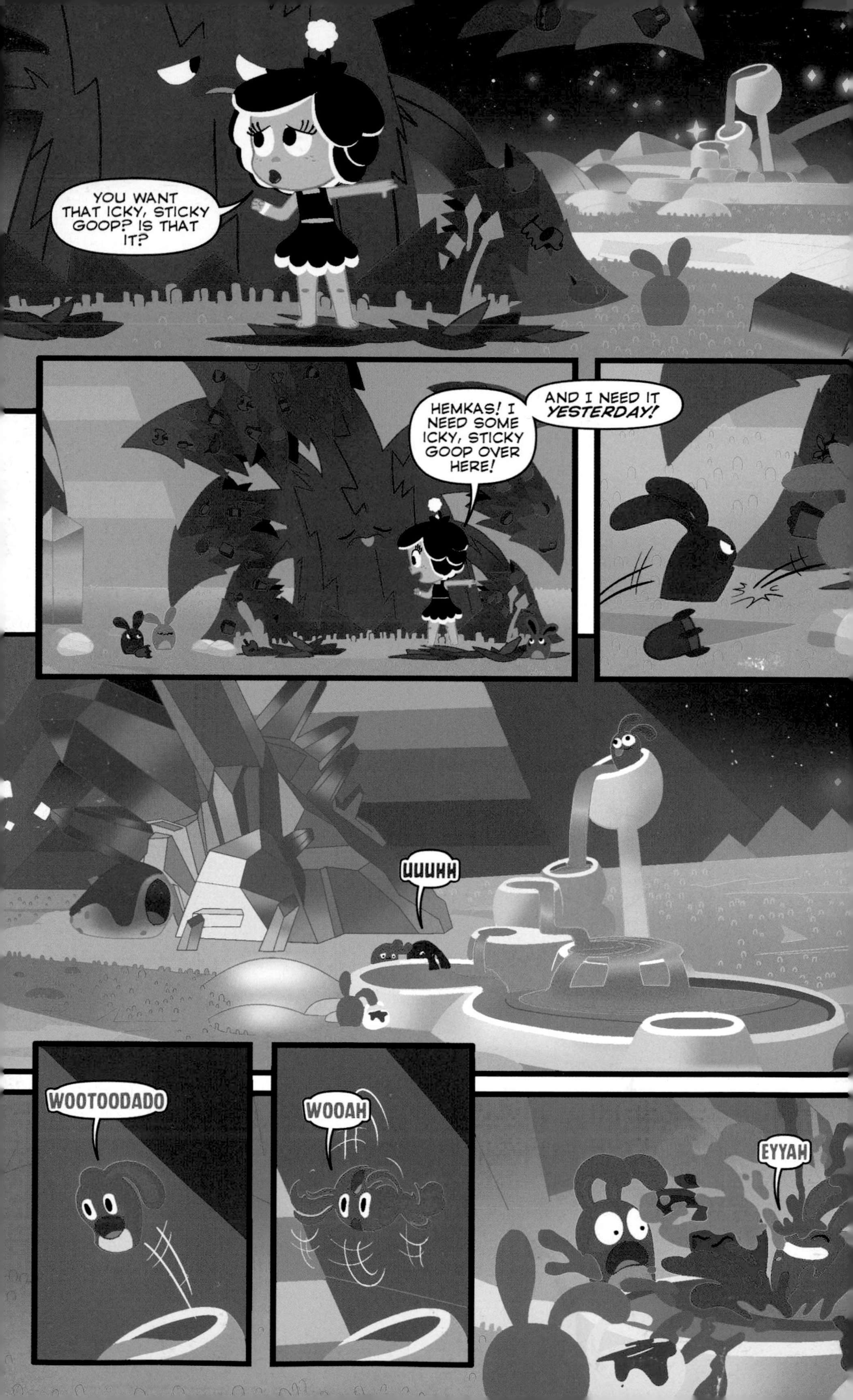
YOU WANT THAT ICKY, STICKY GOOP? IS THAT IT?
HEMKAS! I NEED SOME ICKY, STICKY GOOP OVER HERE!
AND I NEED IT *YESTERDAY!*
UUUHH
WOOTOODADO
WOOAH
EYYAH

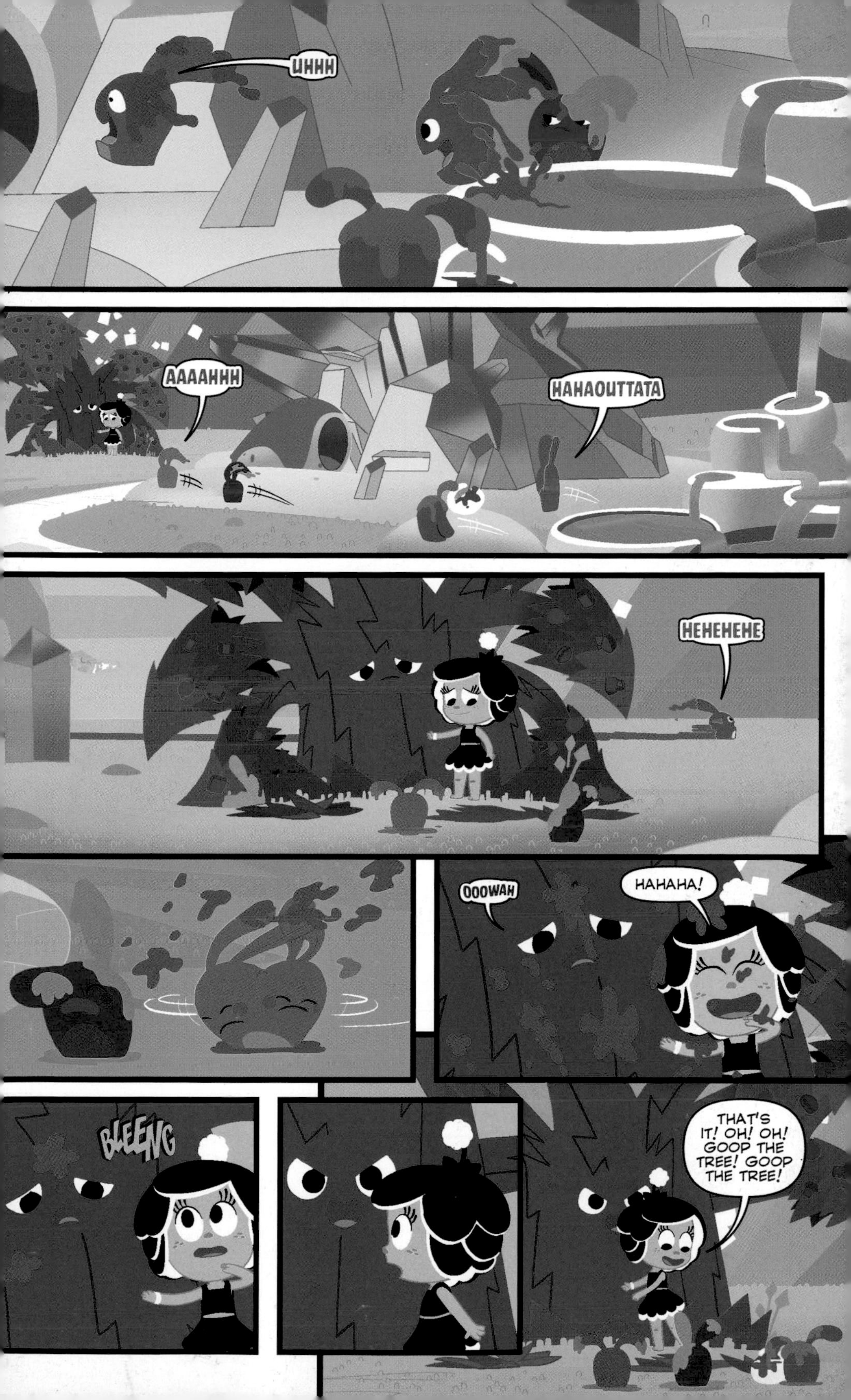
UHHH
AAAAHHH
HAHAOUTTATA
HEHEHEHE
OOOWAH
HAHAHA!
BLEENG
THAT'S IT! OH! OH! GOOP THE TREE! GOOP THE TREE!

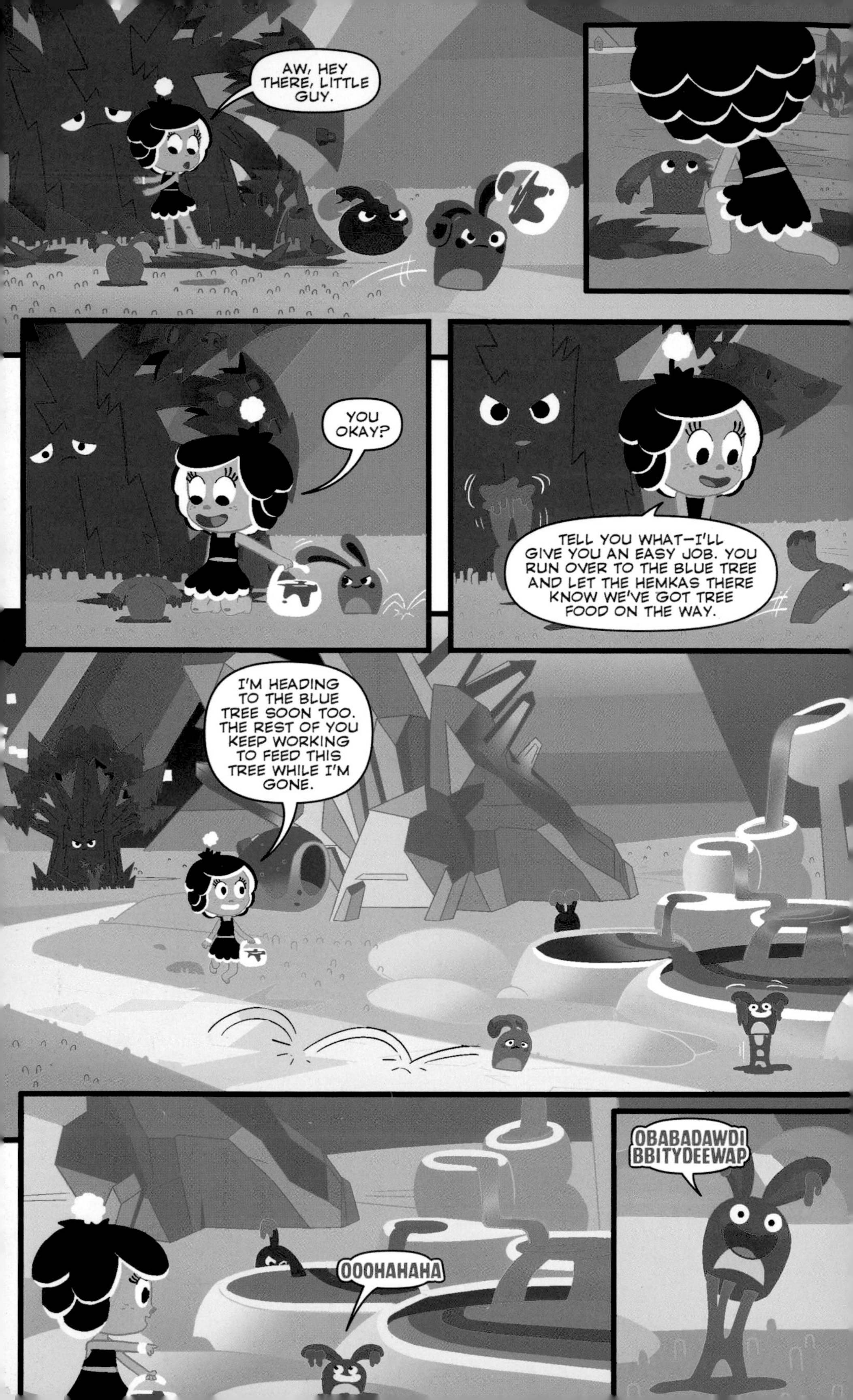
AW, HEY THERE, LITTLE GUY.
YOU OKAY?
TELL YOU WHAT—I'LL GIVE YOU AN EASY JOB. YOU RUN OVER TO THE BLUE TREE AND LET THE HEMKAS THERE KNOW WE'VE GOT TREE FOOD ON THE WAY.
I'M HEADING TO THE BLUE TREE SOON TOO. THE REST OF YOU KEEP WORKING TO FEED THIS TREE WHILE I'M GONE.
OOOHAHAHA
OBABADAWDI BBITYDEEWAP

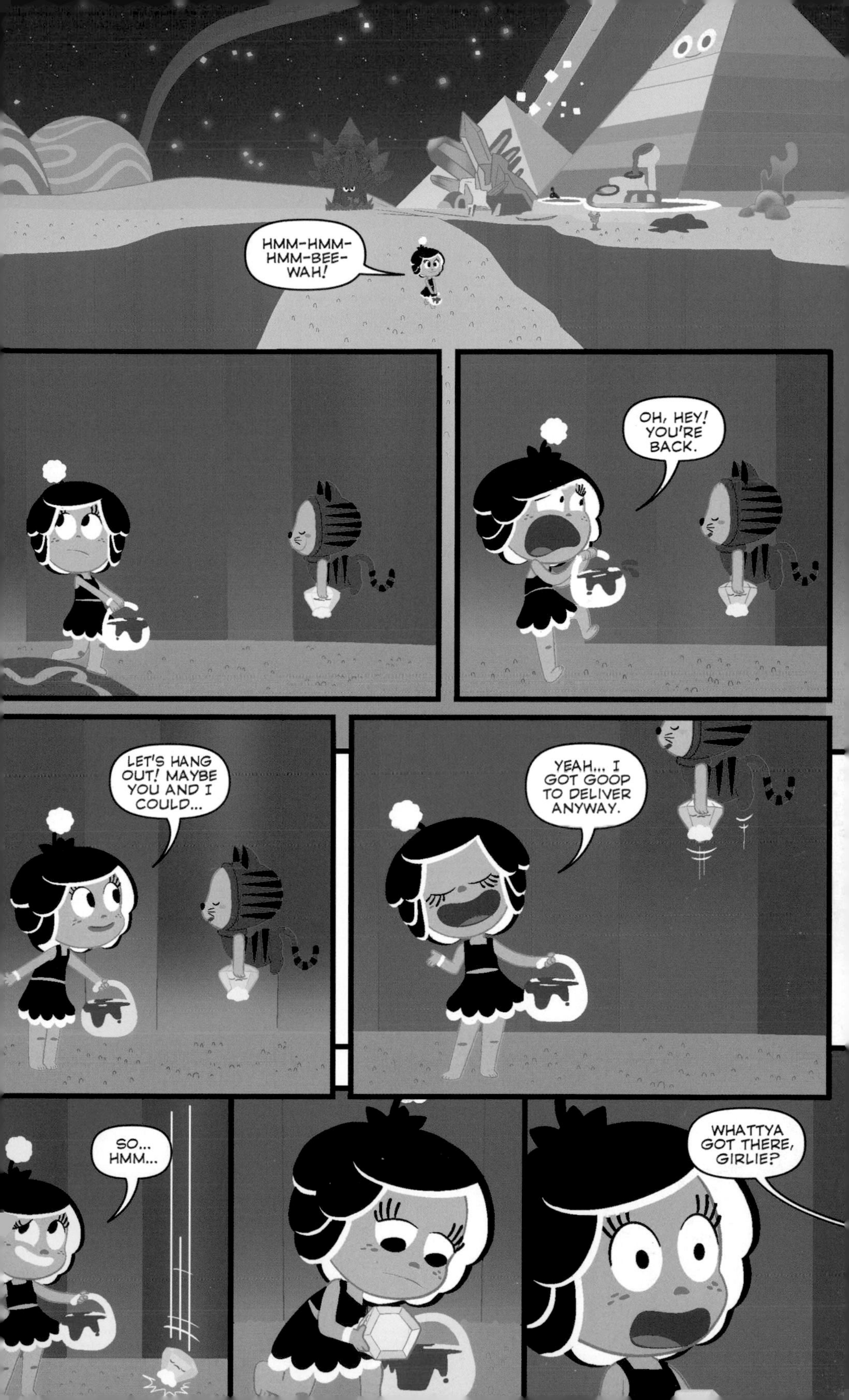
HMM-HMM-HMM-BEE-WAH!
OH, HEY! YOU'RE BACK.
LET'S HANG OUT! MAYBE YOU AND I COULD...
YEAH... I GOT GOOP TO DELIVER ANYWAY.
SO... HMM...
WHATTYA GOT THERE, GIRLIE?

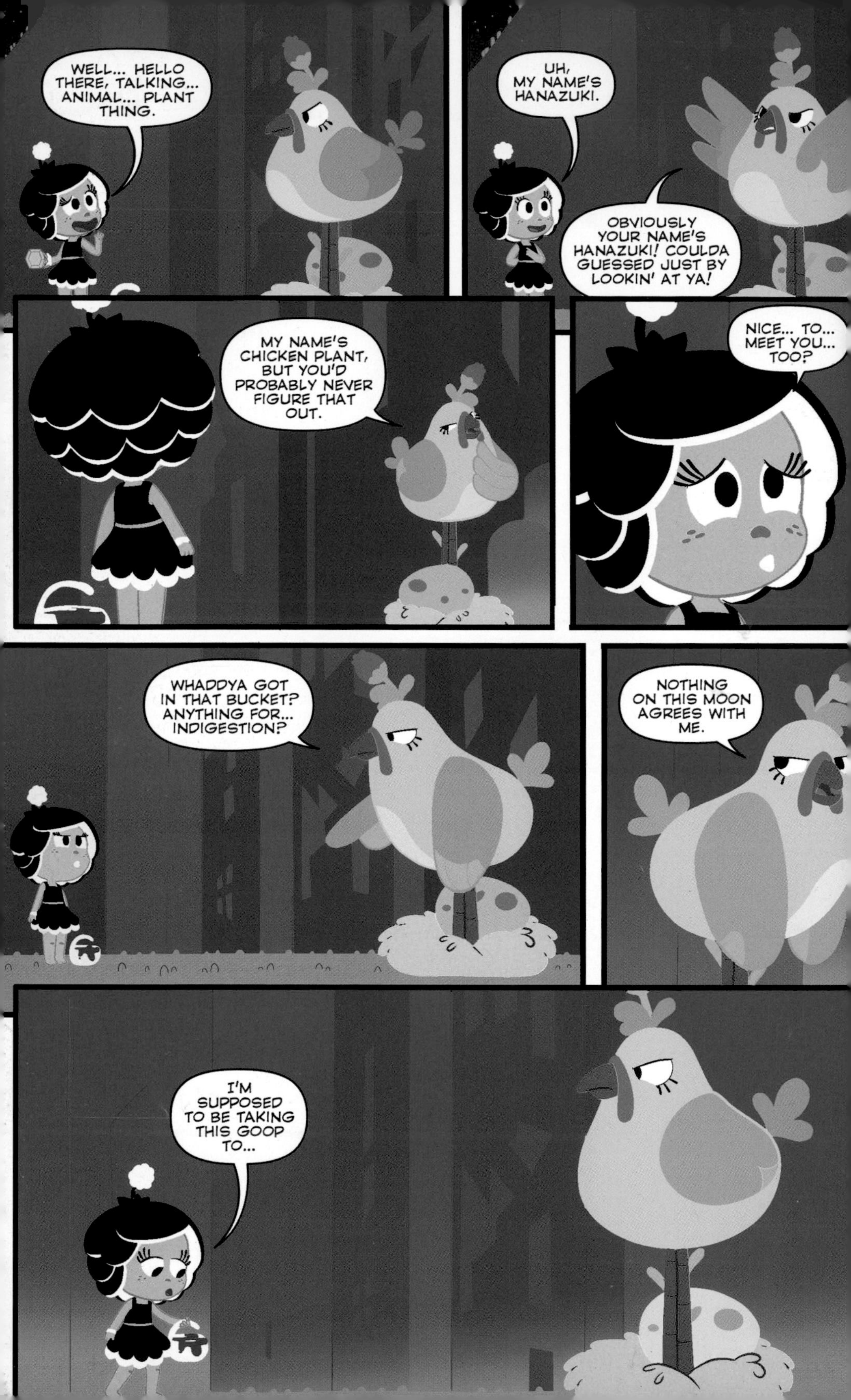
WELL... HELLO THERE, TALKING... ANIMAL... PLANT THING.
UH, MY NAME'S HANAZUKI.
OBVIOUSLY YOUR NAME'S HANAZUKI! COULDA GUESSED JUST BY LOOKIN' AT YA!
MY NAME'S CHICKEN PLANT, BUT YOU'D PROBABLY NEVER FIGURE THAT OUT.
NICE... TO... MEET YOU... TOO?
WHADDYA GOT IN THAT BUCKET? ANYTHING FOR... INDIGESTION?
NOTHING ON THIS MOON AGREES WITH ME.
I'M SUPPOSED TO BE TAKING THIS GOOP TO...

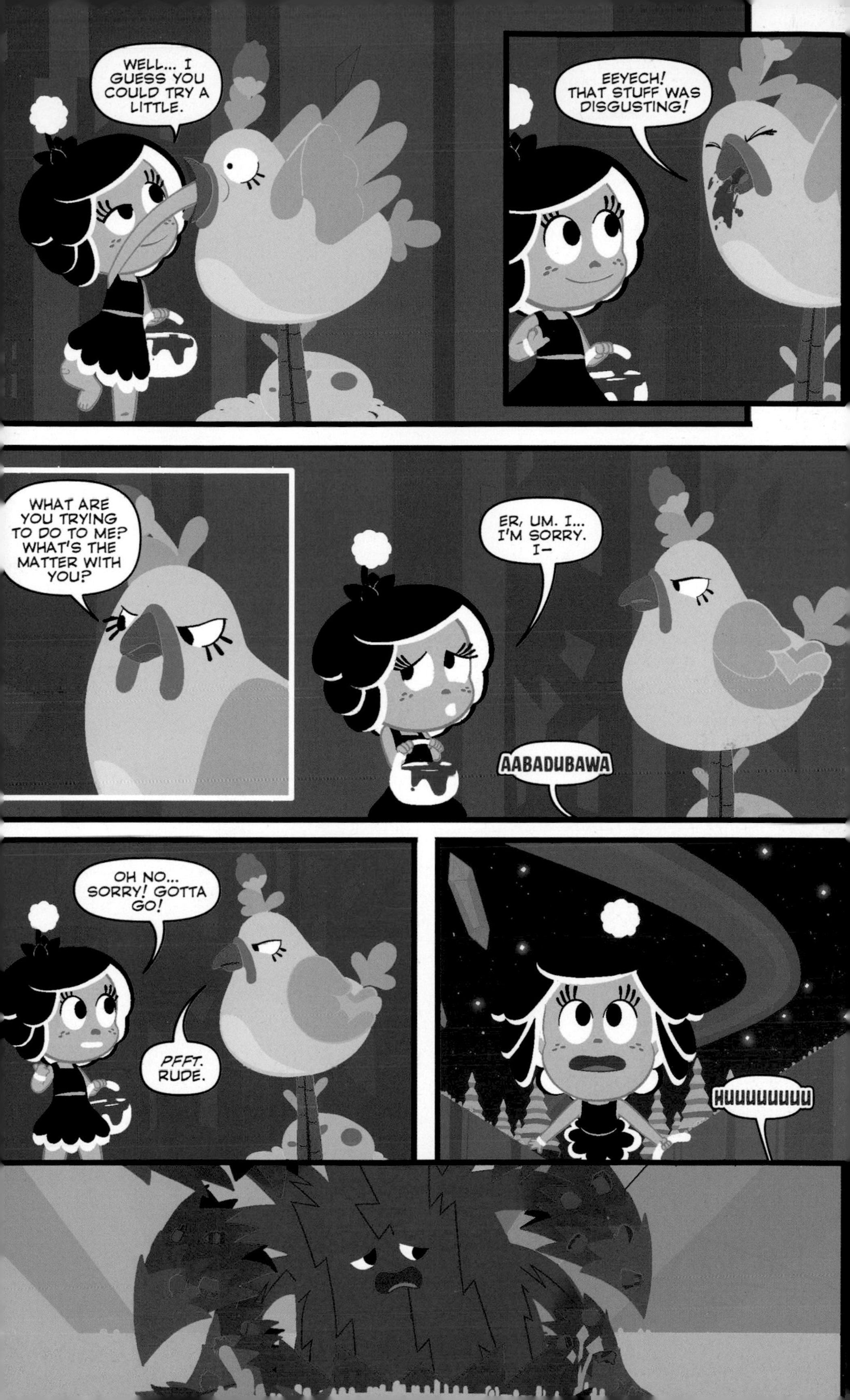
WELL... I GUESS YOU COULD TRY A LITTLE.
EEYECH! THAT STUFF WAS DISGUSTING!
WHAT ARE YOU TRYING TO DO TO ME? WHAT'S THE MATTER WITH YOU?
ER, UM. I... I'M SORRY. I—
AABADUBAWA
OH NO... SORRY! GOTTA GO!
PFFT. RUDE.
HUUUUUUUU

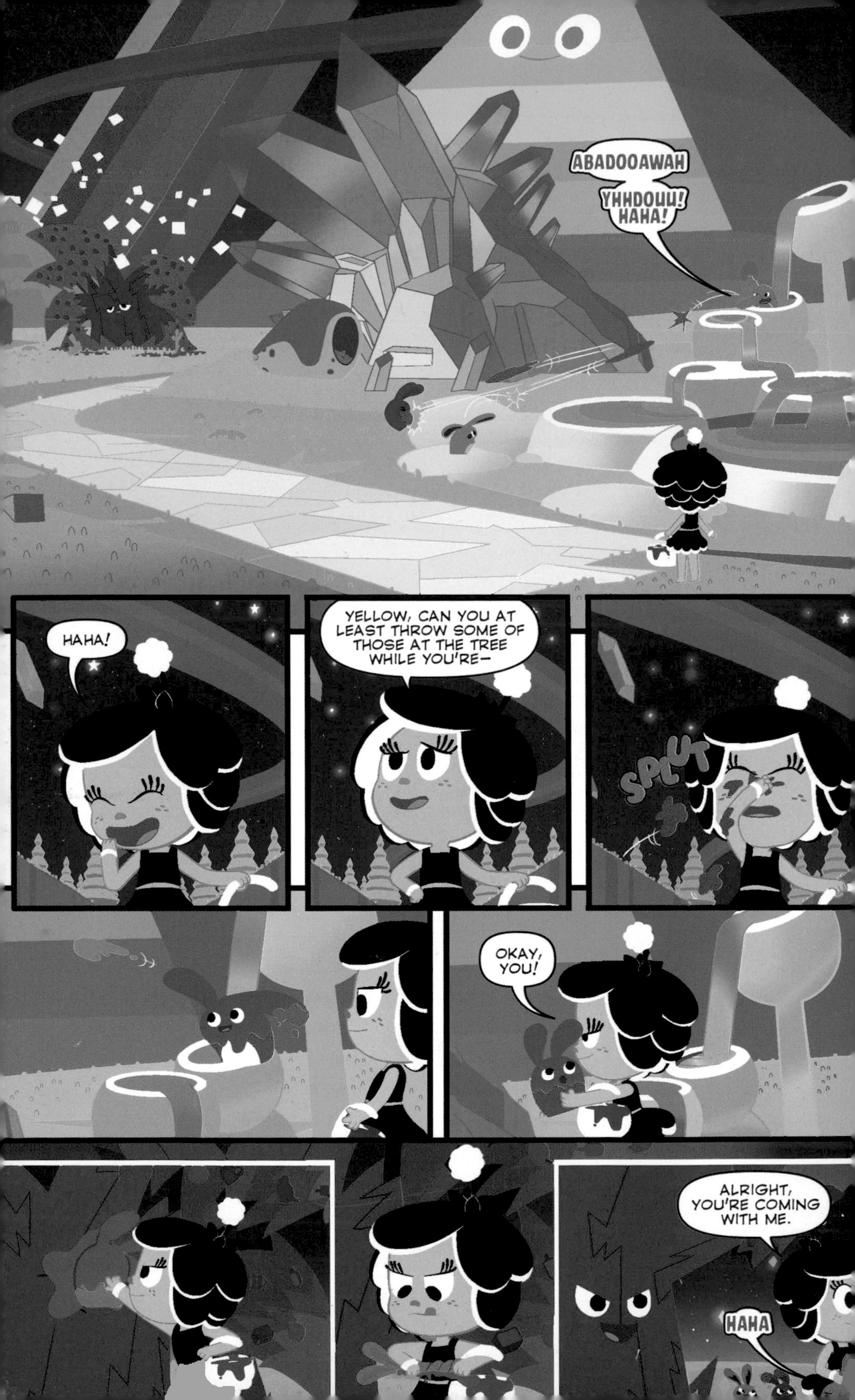
ABADOOAWAH
YHHDOUU! HAHA!
HAHA!
YELLOW, CAN YOU AT LEAST THROW SOME OF THOSE AT THE TREE WHILE YOU'RE—
SPLUT
OKAY, YOU!
ALRIGHT, YOU'RE COMING WITH ME.
HAHA

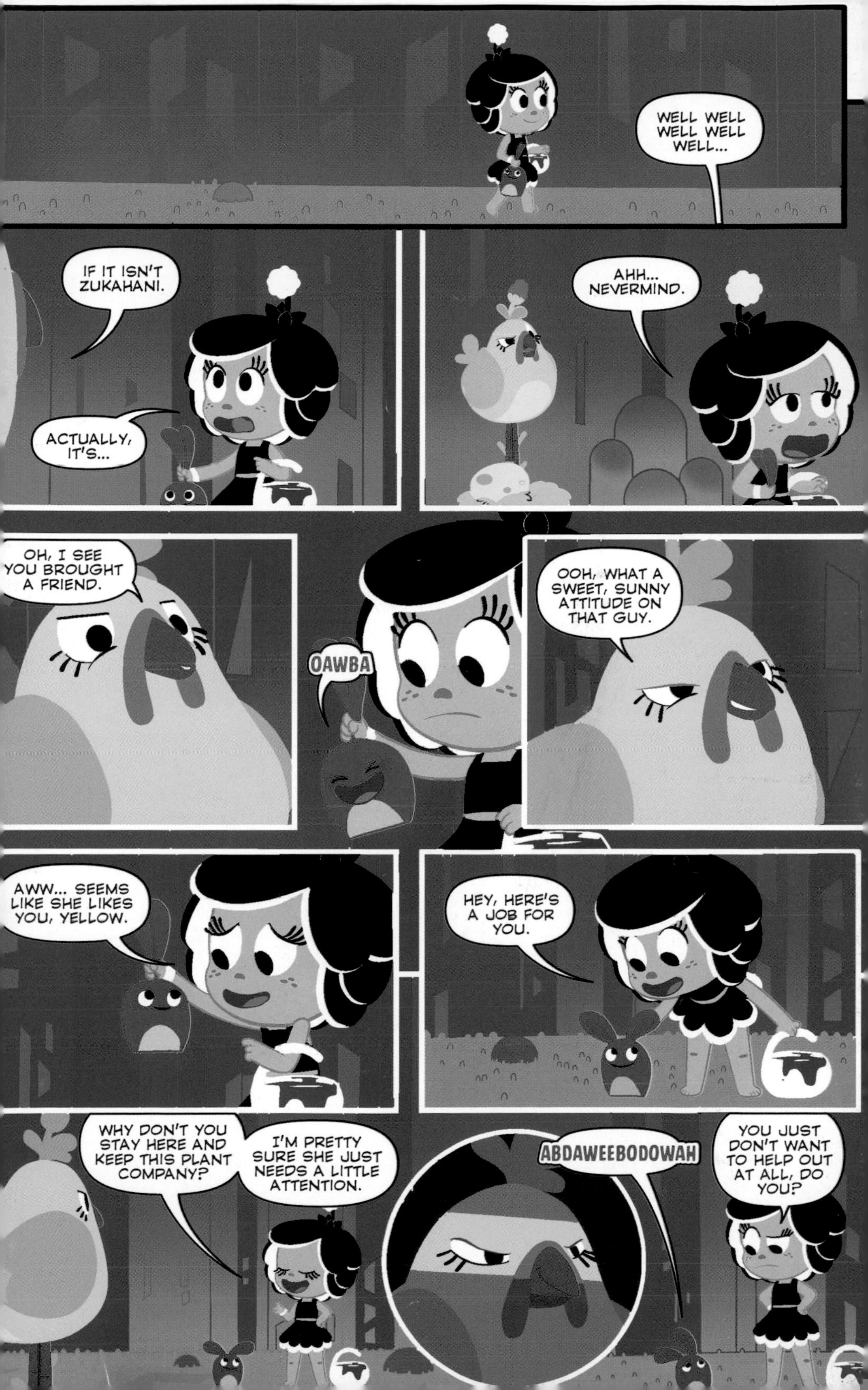
WELL WELL WELL WELL WELL...
IF IT ISN'T ZUKAHANI.
ACTUALLY, IT'S...
AHH... NEVERMIND.
OH, I SEE YOU BROUGHT A FRIEND.
OAWBA
OOH, WHAT A SWEET, SUNNY ATTITUDE ON THAT GUY.
AWW... SEEMS LIKE SHE LIKES YOU, YELLOW.
HEY, HERE'S A JOB FOR YOU.
WHY DON'T YOU STAY HERE AND KEEP THIS PLANT COMPANY?
I'M PRETTY SURE SHE JUST NEEDS A LITTLE ATTENTION.
ABDAWEEBODOWAH
YOU JUST DON'T WANT TO HELP OUT AT ALL, DO YOU?

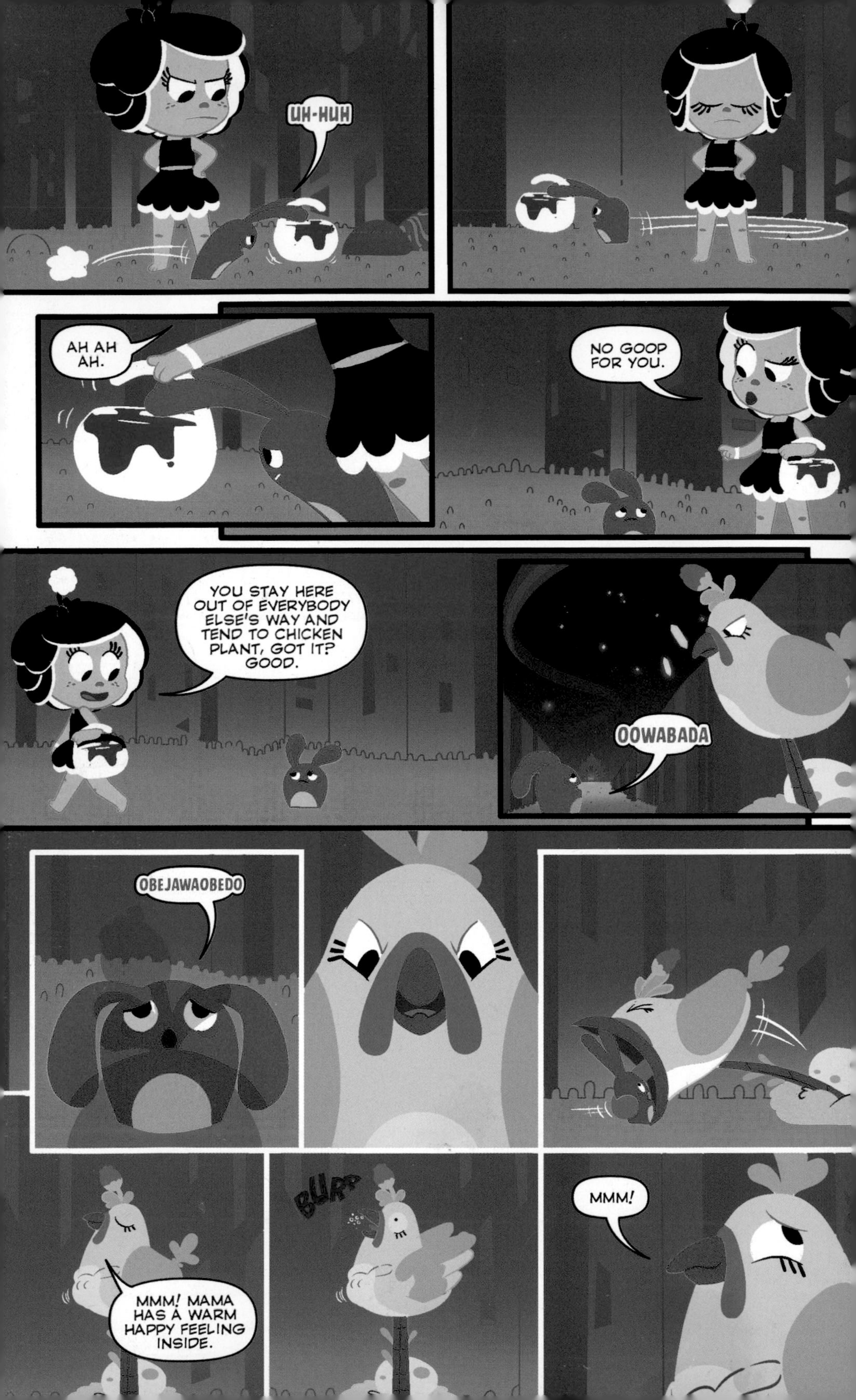
UH-HUH
AH AH AH.
NO GOOP FOR YOU.
YOU STAY HERE OUT OF EVERYBODY ELSE'S WAY AND TEND TO CHICKEN PLANT, GOT IT? GOOD.
OOWABADA
OBEJAWAOBEDO
MMM! MAMA HAS A WARM HAPPY FEELING INSIDE.
BURP
MMM!

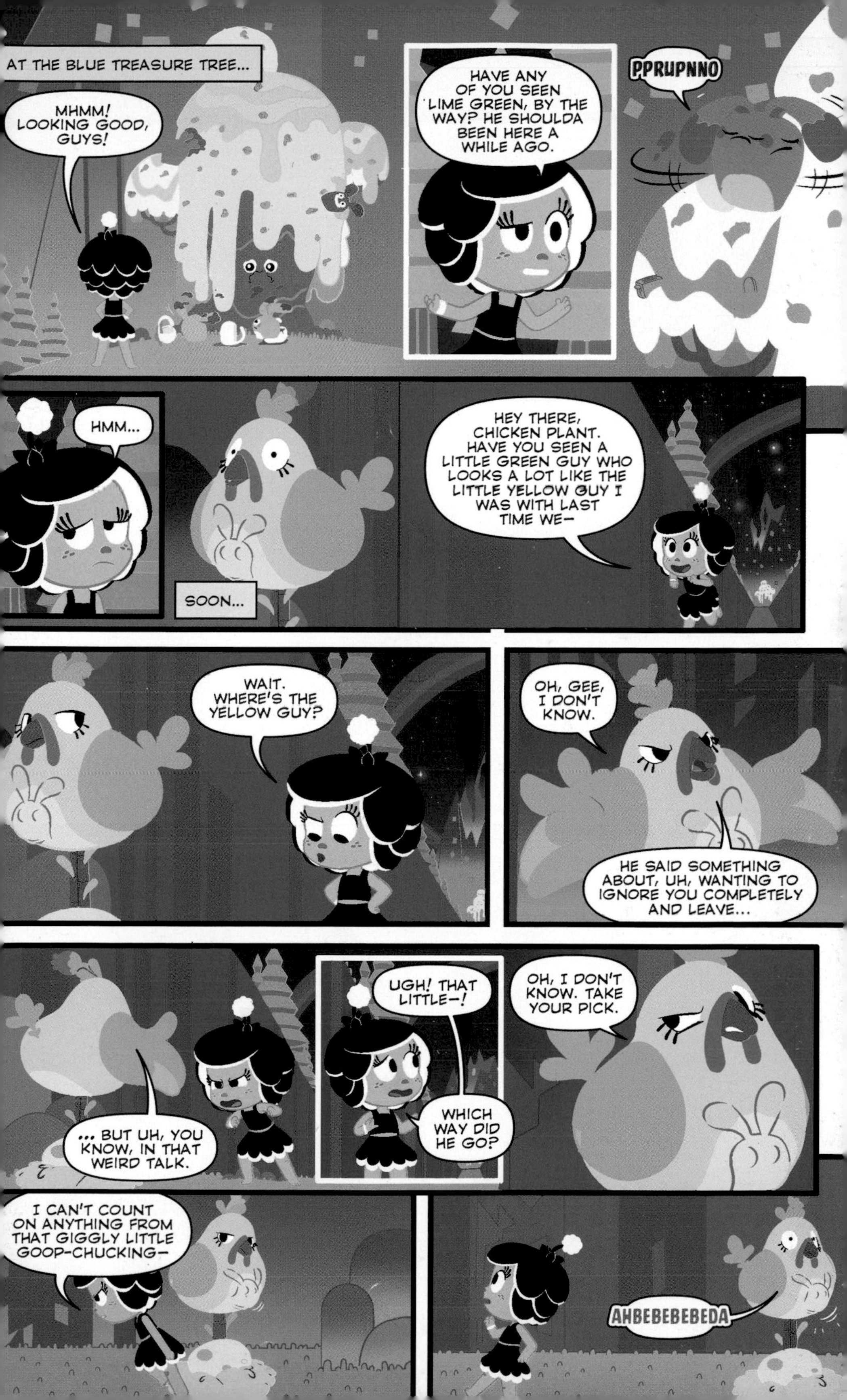
AT THE BLUE TREASURE TREE...
MHMM! LOOKING GOOD, GUYS!
HAVE ANY OF YOU SEEN LIME GREEN, BY THE WAY? HE SHOULDA BEEN HERE A WHILE AGO.
PPRUPNNO
HMM...
SOON...
HEY THERE, CHICKEN PLANT. HAVE YOU SEEN A LITTLE GREEN GUY WHO LOOKS A LOT LIKE THE LITTLE YELLOW GUY I WAS WITH LAST TIME WE—
WAIT. WHERE'S THE YELLOW GUY?
OH, GEE, I DON'T KNOW.
HE SAID SOMETHING ABOUT, UH, WANTING TO IGNORE YOU COMPLETELY AND LEAVE...
... BUT UH, YOU KNOW, IN THAT WEIRD TALK.
UGH! THAT LITTLE—!
WHICH WAY DID HE GO?
OH, I DON'T KNOW. TAKE YOUR PICK.
I CAN'T COUNT ON ANYTHING FROM THAT GIGGLY LITTLE GOOP-CHUCKING—
AHBEBEBEBEDA

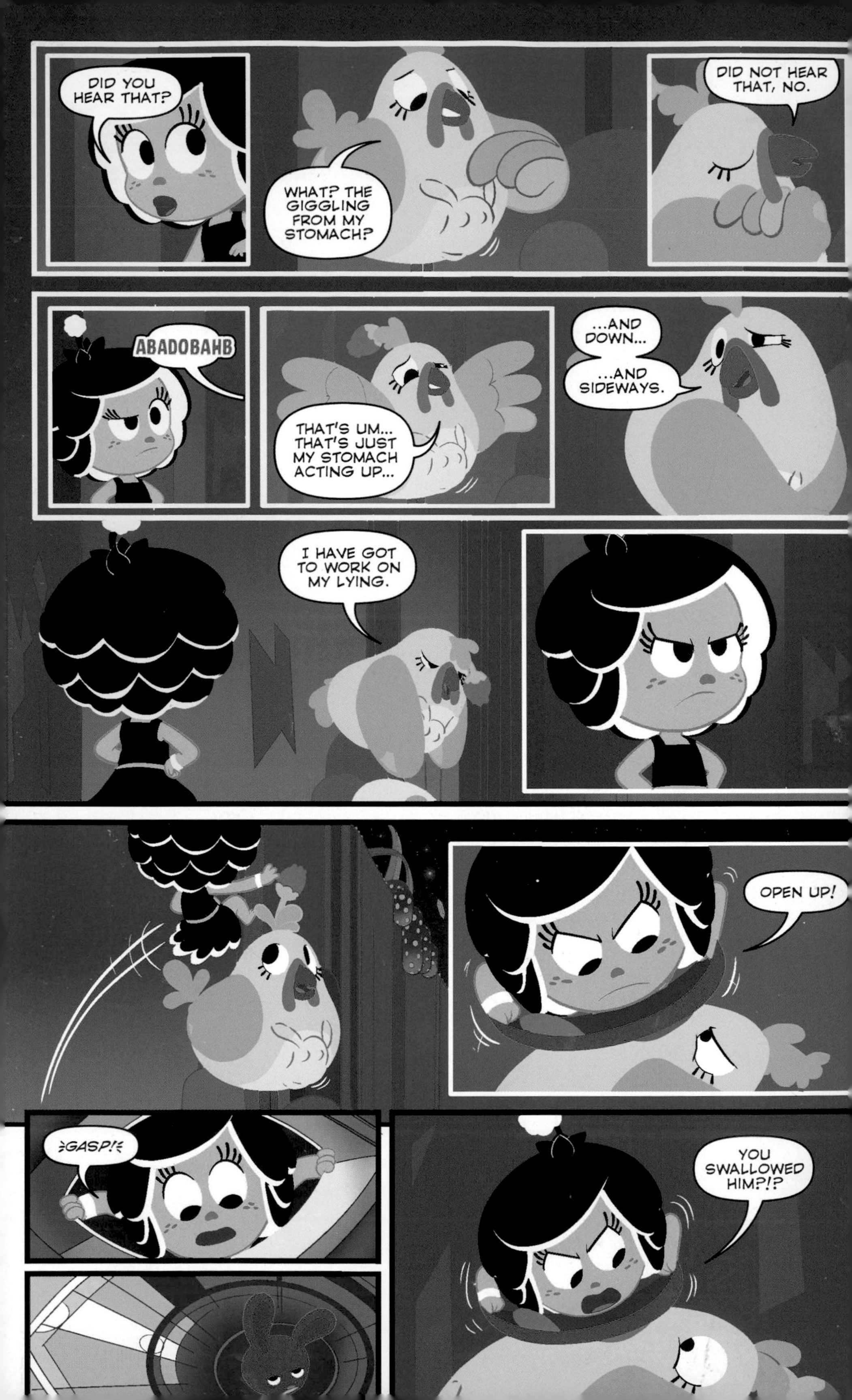
DID YOU HEAR THAT?
WHAT? THE GIGGLING FROM MY STOMACH?
DID NOT HEAR THAT, NO.
ABADOBAHB
THAT'S UM... THAT'S JUST MY STOMACH ACTING UP...
...AND DOWN...
...AND SIDEWAYS.
I HAVE GOT TO WORK ON MY LYING.
OPEN UP!
GASP!
YOU SWALLOWED HIM?!?

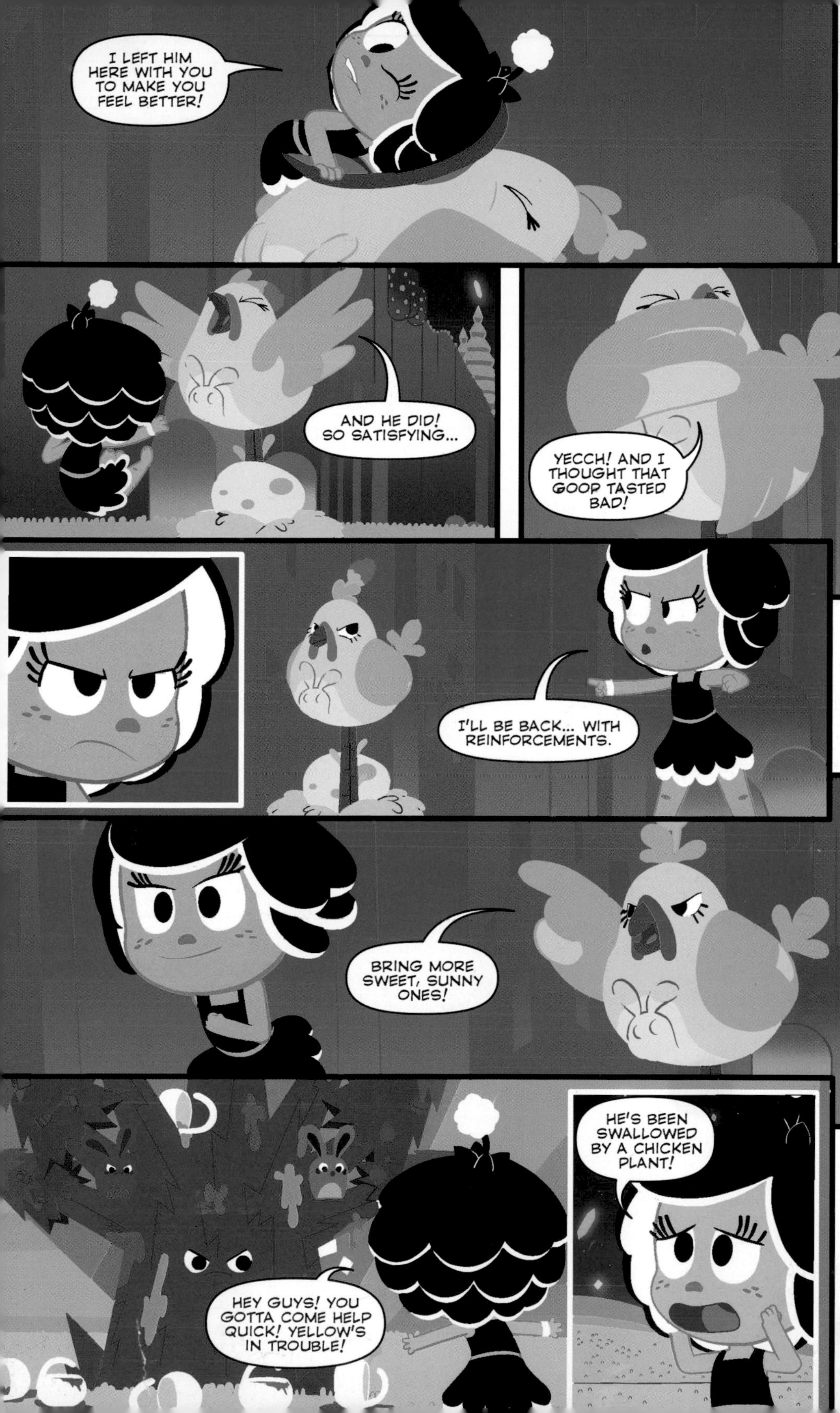
I LEFT HIM HERE WITH YOU TO MAKE YOU FEEL BETTER!
AND HE DID! SO SATISFYING...
YECCH! AND I THOUGHT THAT GOOP TASTED BAD!
I'LL BE BACK... WITH REINFORCEMENTS.
BRING MORE SWEET, SUNNY ONES!
HEY GUYS! YOU GOTTA COME HELP QUICK! YELLOW'S IN TROUBLE!
HE'S BEEN SWALLOWED BY A CHICKEN PLANT!

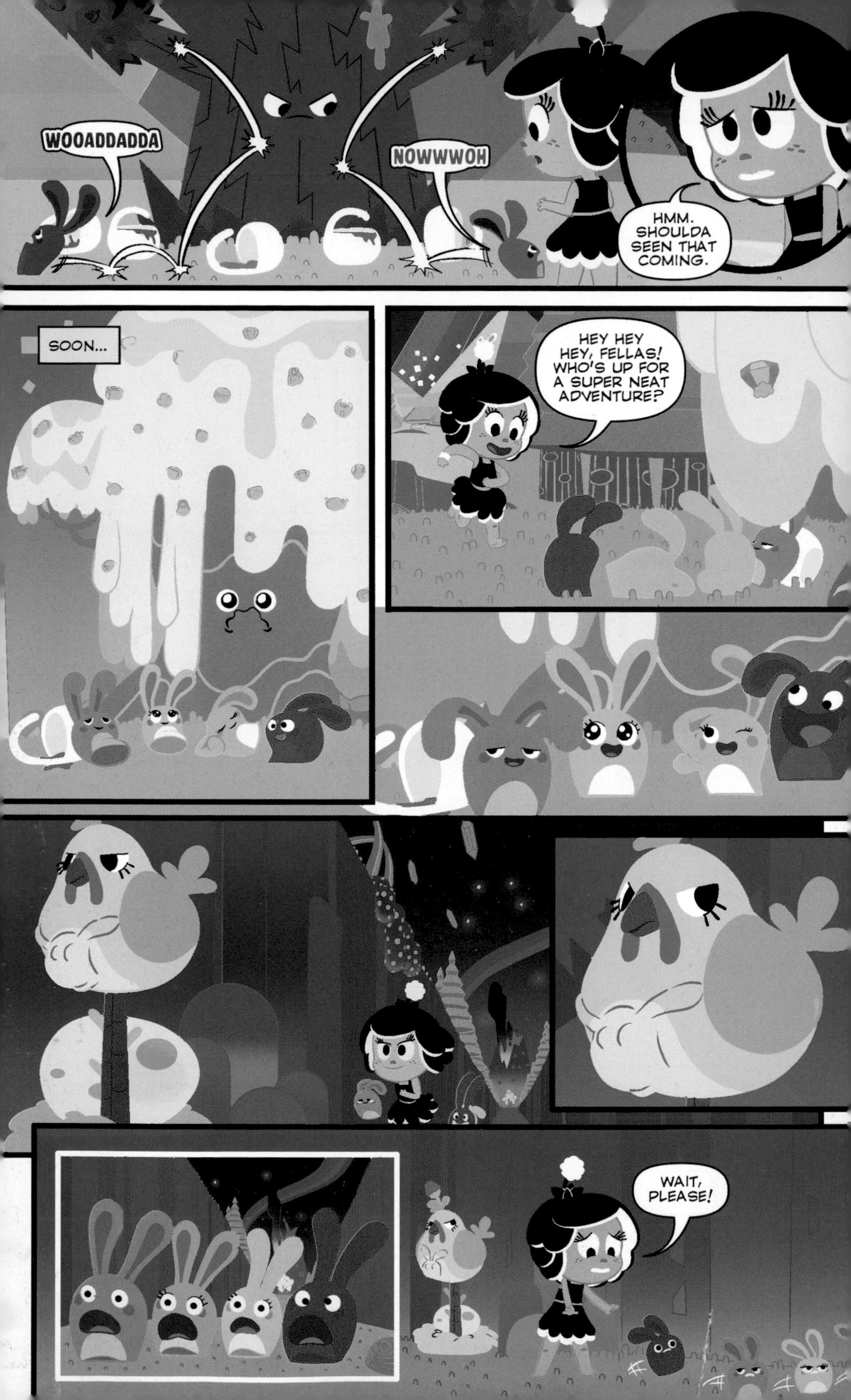
WOOADDADDA
NOWWWOH
HMM. SHOULDA SEEN THAT COMING.
SOON...
HEY HEY HEY, FELLAS! WHO'S UP FOR A SUPER NEAT ADVENTURE?
WAIT, PLEASE!

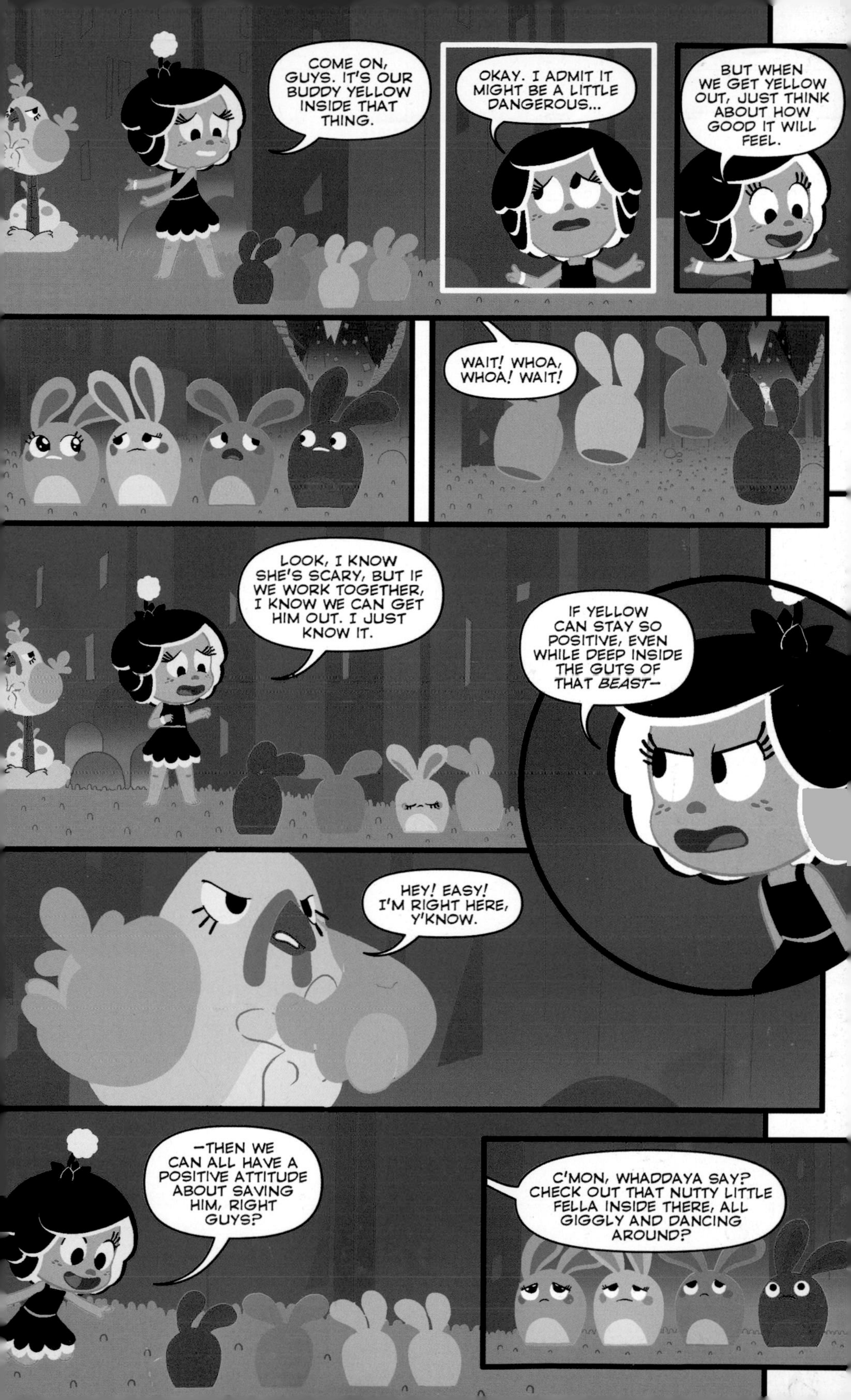
COME ON, GUYS. IT'S OUR BUDDY YELLOW INSIDE THAT THING.
OKAY. I ADMIT IT MIGHT BE A LITTLE DANGEROUS...
BUT WHEN WE GET YELLOW OUT, JUST THINK ABOUT HOW GOOD IT WILL FEEL.
WAIT! WHOA, WHOA! WAIT!
LOOK, I KNOW SHE'S SCARY, BUT IF WE WORK TOGETHER, I KNOW WE CAN GET HIM OUT. I JUST KNOW IT.
IF YELLOW CAN STAY SO POSITIVE, EVEN WHILE DEEP INSIDE THE GUTS OF THAT *BEAST*—
HEY! EASY! I'M RIGHT HERE, Y'KNOW.
—THEN WE CAN ALL HAVE A POSITIVE ATTITUDE ABOUT SAVING HIM, RIGHT GUYS?
C'MON, WHADDAYA SAY? CHECK OUT THAT NUTTY LITTLE FELLA INSIDE THERE, ALL GIGGLY AND DANCING AROUND?

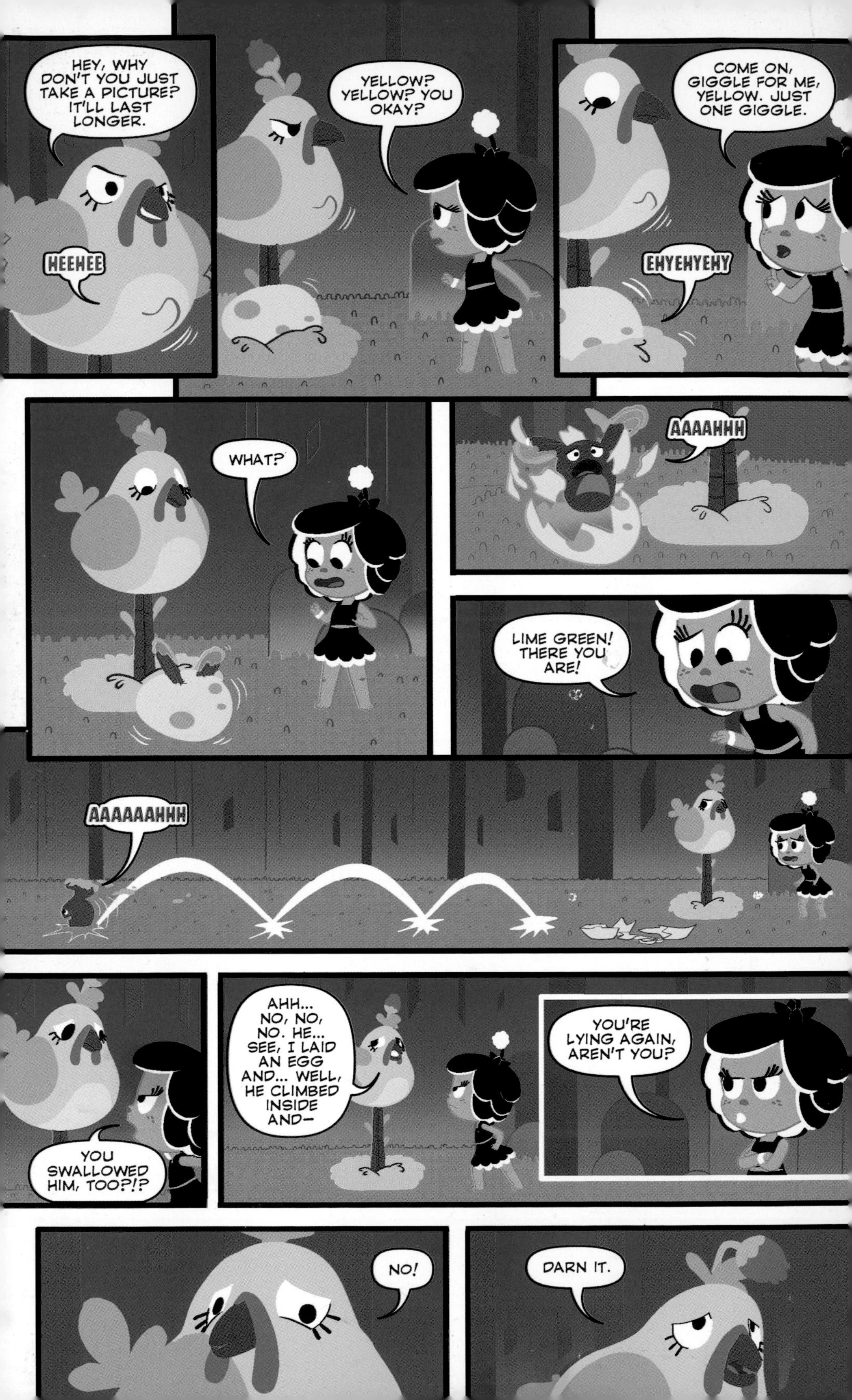
HEY, WHY DON'T YOU JUST TAKE A PICTURE? IT'LL LAST LONGER.
HEEHEE
YELLOW? YELLOW? YOU OKAY?
COME ON, GIGGLE FOR ME, YELLOW. JUST ONE GIGGLE.
EHYEHYEHY
WHAT?
AAAAHHH
LIME GREEN! THERE YOU ARE!
AAAAAAHHH
YOU SWALLOWED HIM, TOO?!?
AHH... NO, NO, NO. HE... SEE, I LAID AN EGG AND... WELL, HE CLIMBED INSIDE AND—
YOU'RE LYING AGAIN, AREN'T YOU?
NO!
DARN IT.

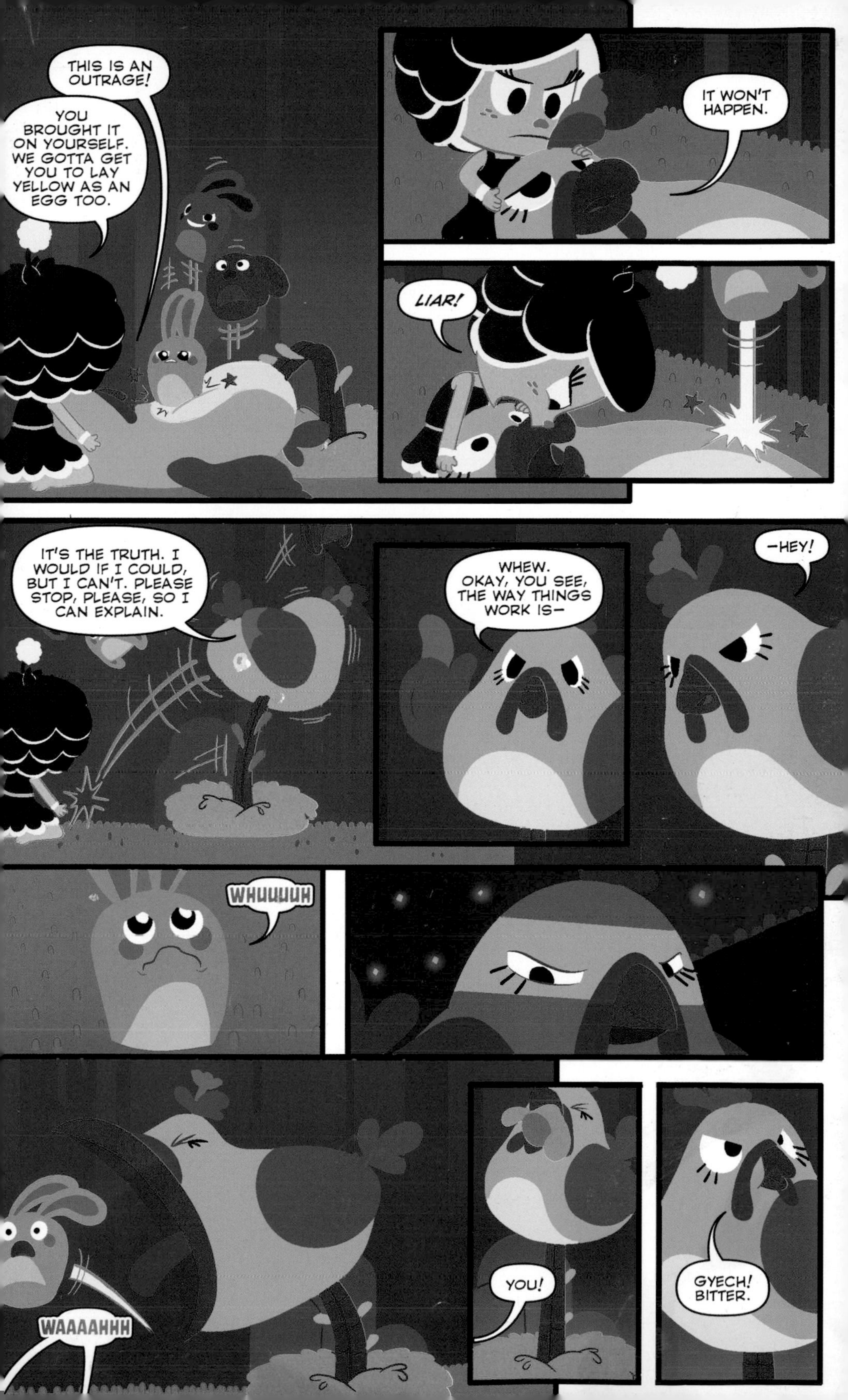
THIS IS AN OUTRAGE!
YOU BROUGHT IT ON YOURSELF. WE GOTTA GET YOU TO LAY YELLOW AS AN EGG TOO.
IT WON'T HAPPEN.
LIAR!
IT'S THE TRUTH. I WOULD IF I COULD, BUT I CAN'T. PLEASE STOP, PLEASE, SO I CAN EXPLAIN.
WHEW. OKAY, YOU SEE, THE WAY THINGS WORK IS—
—HEY!
WHUUUUH
WAAAAHHH
YOU!
GYECH! BITTER.

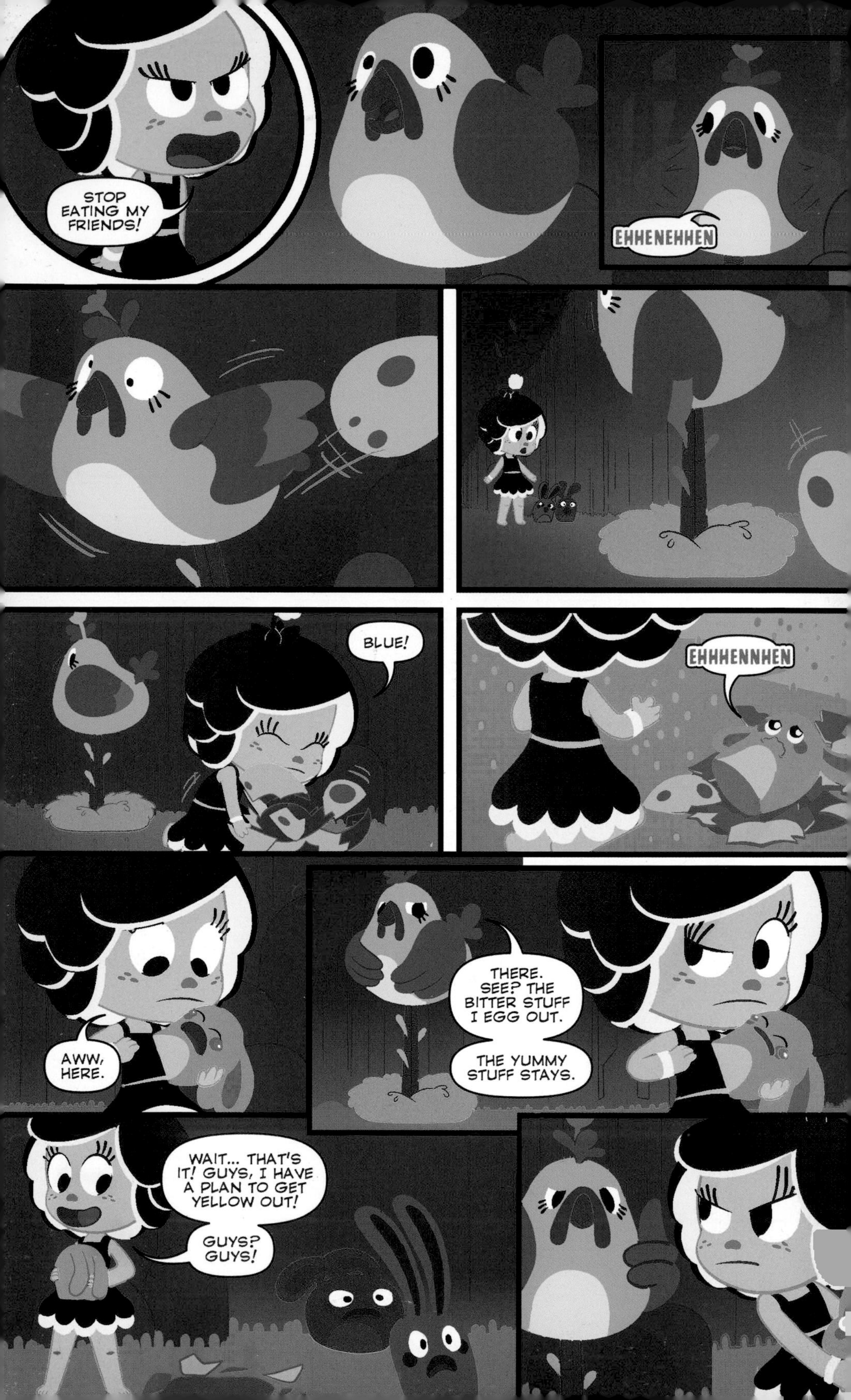
STOP EATING MY FRIENDS!
EHHENEHHEN
BLUE!
EHHHENNHEN
AWW, HERE.
THERE. SEE? THE BITTER STUFF I EGG OUT.
THE YUMMY STUFF STAYS.
WAIT... THAT'S IT! GUYS, I HAVE A PLAN TO GET YELLOW OUT!
GUYS? GUYS!

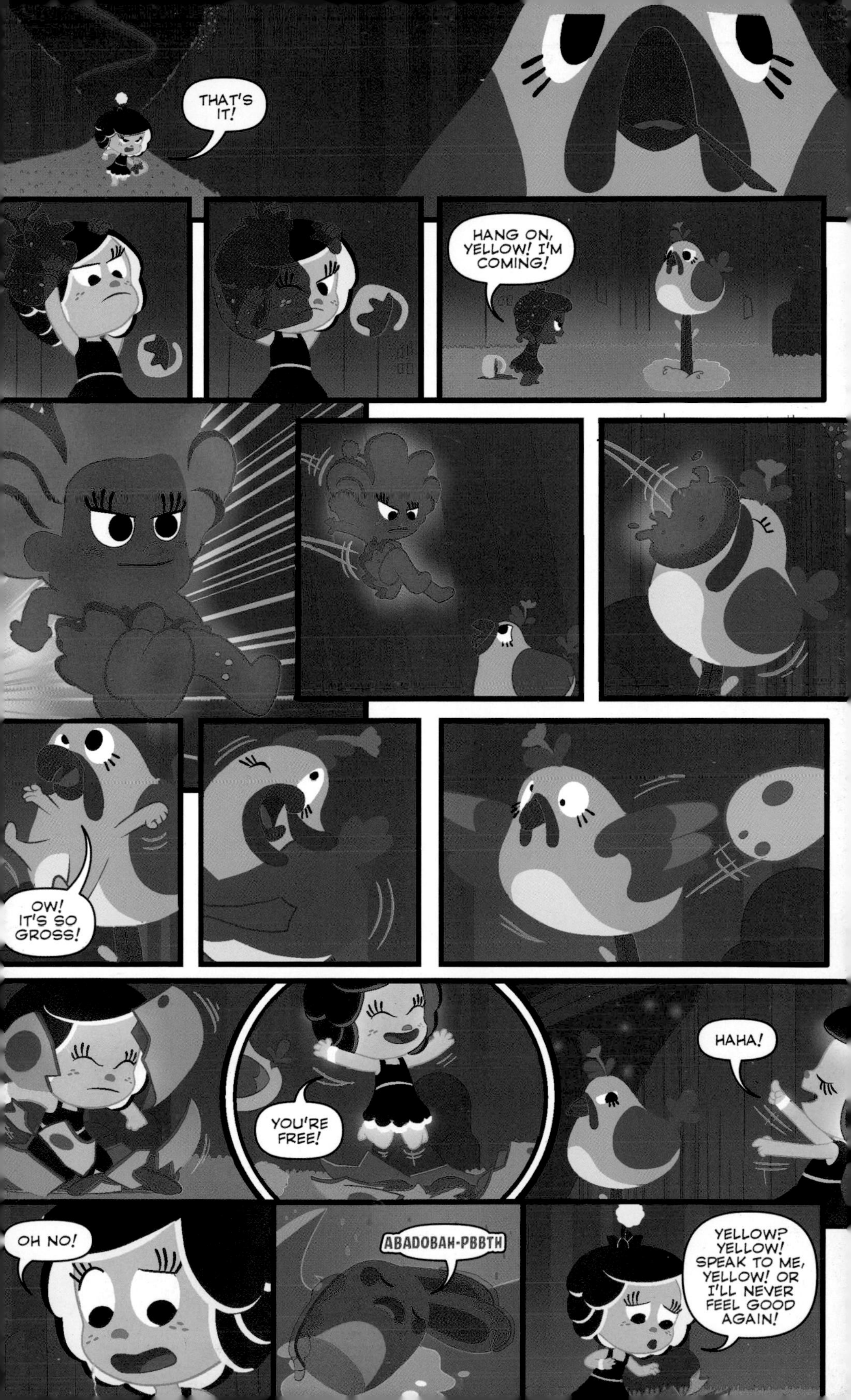

THAT'S IT!
HANG ON, YELLOW! I'M COMING!
OW! IT'S SO GROSS!
YOU'RE FREE!
HAHA!
OH NO!
ABADOBAH-PBBTH
YELLOW? YELLOW! SPEAK TO ME, YELLOW! OR I'LL NEVER FEEL GOOD AGAIN!

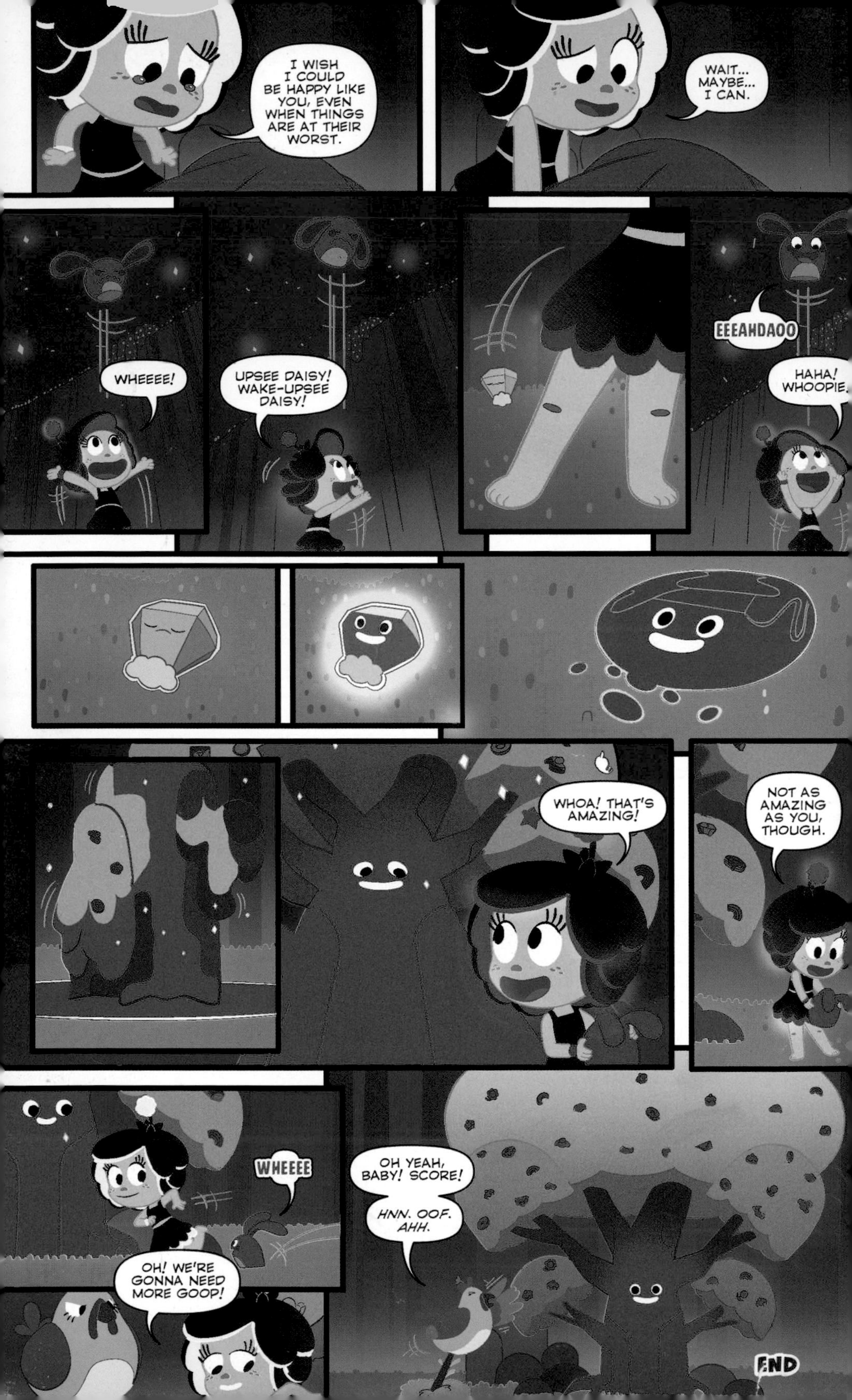
I WISH I COULD BE HAPPY LIKE YOU, EVEN WHEN THINGS ARE AT THEIR WORST.
WAIT... MAYBE... I CAN.
WHEEEE!
UPSEE DAISY! WAKE-UPSEE DAISY!
EEEAHDAOO
HAHA! WHOOPIE.
WHOA! THAT'S AMAZING!
NOT AS AMAZING AS YOU, THOUGH.
WHEEEE
OH! WE'RE GONNA NEED MORE GOOP!
OH YEAH, BABY! SCORE!
HNN. OOF. AHH.
END